HML Writers
Volume 1

Dedication

Without the support of Tina Winstead, the director of the Huntington Memorial Library, and without the regular attendance of my writers, this anthology never would have happened. I am so very grateful for everybody's dedication; this anthology contains the first publication for several writers, and I am proud to be able to share them with the world.

HML Writers was first started in July of 2014, using the framework of Camp National Novel Writing Month (Camp NaNoWriMo), the summer sister of the November-based National Novel Writing Month. HML Writers still has its summer session in July, but has expanded beyond the NaNoWriMo family and into a longer-running workshop series. Writers bring what they're working on to read out loud, or pass out copies for critique. More often than not, most of the meeting time is devoted to the act of writing, with timers set and prompts given as a springboard for a story or poem to take flight.

We're not all novelists, or poets, or short-story writers. We're not all speed writers; trying to go-go-go on a prompt for 10 minutes isn't everybody's writing style. And that's all right. The goal for HML Writers is to help writers be comfortable with themselves, with their own styles and their own needs. Has everybody who signed up for our NaNoWriMo styled sessions written a novel? No. And it doesn't matter.

What matters is some of my participants are writing again, after having spent years without doing so creatively. What matters is some of my participants are trying it out for the first time. Some are writing for their children. Some are writing with publication in mind. The intent is to welcome writers of all styles, and foster an environment where we can talk about our goals, our troubles, and our successes. We talk about the need to write, and about giving ourselves permission to take our writing seriously, and take ourselves seriously as writers. We talk about where stories come from. This anthology is the result of all that dedication and hard work.

Table of Contents

Back Up Plan
Jamie McNamara

M onday morning. Again. So soon. I get up reluctantly. "Good Morning, cats," I say to Kitty and Tommy, my two formerly stray cats. I realize that they are not very original names, and think again to myself, "It's a good thing I never had children. I would have been too lazy to give them names. They might have ended up in school being called Boy and Girl. And they might have turned out to be serial killers, and it would have been all my fault. Just what the world needs, more maladjusted serial killers. Actually I suppose there aren't many well-adjusted serial killers. And the blame always goes back to the mother."

Tommy makes a distressed cat noise and jumps onto the bed next to me. Kitty jumps up on my other side. I think about their names, or lack of, and realize that I had never intended to keep them I had found them during a blizzard three years ago, and fully intended to take them to the animal shelter, when it opened. But I never got around to it, and so I never consciously named them. It was only when I found myself replying "sure, why not" when the young sales clerk at Petco asked me if I wanted to apply for a frequent shopper rewards card, that I knew it was a done deal. The cats were now officially mine. I took them to the vet for shots, and to be spayed and neutered. And then I threw out the sticky note with the animal shelter's phone number on it that had been stuck to my refrigerator since the snowy rescue.

Of course that kind of thoughtless procrastination would not work with children. They won't let you leave the hospital without a name on the birth certificate. Cats were about as much responsibility as I could handle. You never have to send them to college. Or let them borrow the car. And you won't get arrested if you should leave them alone while on a two night bender.

I scratch each cat on the head lightly, not wanting to show favoritism. I might be lazy and thoughtless, but I believe I am fair. If I had raised two serial killers at least the tabloids could report that I had been fair. But was it really possible not to show a preference for one child over another? So maybe I would have raised only one serial killer. But that is not the point right now. Right now I have to get to work.

I need to focus and stop these inane ramblings. Once again I am scrambling to get ready for work. I have to find something relatively clean, not totally covered in cat hair. The chair in the corner of my bedroom holds some possibilities. I rummage through the pile for something semi-presentable. Of course if I had done some laundry over the weekend, I wouldn't have this problem. If I had done anything constructive over the weekend, I would not be in panic mode yet again. Hindsight allowed me to see that a wine tasting marathon was probably not the best way to spend the weekend.

After settling on my outfit, I head for the bathroom. Looking at the woman in the mirror, I wince.Note to self; do not color your hair, or tweeze your eyebrows when you have been drinking. I wipe off the smeared mascara and twist up my multi-hued hair into a knot behind my head and fasten it with a clasp, trying to contain it somehow. The worst of the broad, brassy, blond strip is mostly out of sight.

After some coffee, aspirin, and mouthwash, I am ready. I hope they are. I think of their shining little faces, all lined up in the classroom, watching me. I sigh so loudly that the cats turn to look at me.

"Wish me luck guys. I'm off. Somebody has to bring home the Meow Mix."

I had never intended teaching as a career. After college I believed I was going to set the world on fire with my brilliant prose. My first novel would take the literary world by storm. But on the advice of my parents I reluctantly agreed to get my certification for teaching.

"It's something you can always fall back on," advised my ever-so-sensible mother.

I scoffed. There would be no falling back in my future. I had been young and confident and perhaps a bit arrogant. But Mom and Dad had paid for a good bit of my tuition and so I acquiesced. Now here I was, thirty two years later heading to my classroom, to impart my brilliance to a bunch of eleven year olds who couldn't care less.

Had I been like these little savages when I was their age? Who the hell could remember? I do remember liking some of my teachers and really detesting others. I was under no illusion which category my students would put me into. Oh, what difference does it make? It's a paycheck.

I head out the door with my fortified tea in my travel mug. The cats silently watch me go. I wonder if they are glad to be rid of me. Here I go, stepping onto that treadmill of crushing sameness, the same drive, the same room, and the same kids. I can't remember all of their names. Some of the names stood out, and therefore some of the children stood out. But I couldn't say that was necessarily a good thing. In the last two years I had had two girls named Destiny, a boy named Jupiter and a girl named Beauty. Talk about setting up your kid for disappointment. All parents want their children to be unique and interesting, but I always believed that if you give a kid a weird name, he'll be a weird kid. I have found this to be mostly true. I sometimes looked out at my little captives and wondered if there were any future criminals waiting to seek revenge on their oblivious parents.

If there were, would I be partly to blame? Well, I was only the teacher, not the mother. Was I even a teacher anymore? These days I just basically showed up, tried to keep some semblance of order in the classroom, and then went home to my sanctuary with my two cats and my two glasses of wine. Sometimes it was three or four and they were pretty big glasses. But I earned it.

There is a new girl in the class. She has only been here for two weeks. She is a little different from the other kids. She actually seems to be thinking sometimes. And her name is Jane. Now there's a throwback. I find myself wondering if she was named for Jane Eyre, or Jane Austen, or Tarzan's Jane. If I spoke to these kids about personal things, I might have asked her. Of course the others had started to call her Plain Jane, or Brain Jane. She is rather bright, but she keeps to herself. This seems to bother the other kids. Today after returning from Art class, they bring their attempts at water colors with them. Michelle, one of the louder girls, is mocking Jane's work, sneering "Did you ever see orange grass? Grass can't be orange. It's green." I always imagine that Michelle has a great career ahead of her as a drill sergeant.

Jane responds by pushing out her lower lip and shrugging her shoulders. She doesn't seem to give a damn. "You go Jane," I think.

"Do you think anyone ever told Picasso that people didn't have both eyes on the same side of their faces?" I ask sharply, looking at Jane's painting. Michelle looks at me with contempt. The feeling is mutual, honey, I think to myself. I look at Jane. Is that the hint of a smile?

Back to our lessons. What had I been trying to teach them? Oh yeah. Sentence structure. To a bunch of kids who communicate in LOL and WTF and emoji's, cave paintings for the 21st century. Oh well, I'm getting paid. Glancing around the room for some spark of interest, I notice that Jane appears to be staring at me. I hesitate on her. She smiles. WTF, I think to myself. I quickly look away.

At the end of another excruciating day, the children stampede out the door. Except Jane, who is standing by my desk looking intently at me. I look back with my teacher glare, the one I hope signals "Keep an appropriate distance."

"Who is Picasso?" she asks.

I am taken aback. "He was a very famous painter, with a unique style."

"Did people laugh at him?"

"Probably, sometimes, but he just went on painting his own way. I could show you some of his pictures. I have a book ...." I catch myself. Did I just say that? I wanted to bite my tongue off.

Her eyes light up. I feel a strange facial twitch.

"Ok, I'll bring it to school. You might like his paintings."

Still, she stands there.

"Ms. Hennessy," says Jane looking at me intently, "Your hair is like three or four different colors."

My head spins to look at her. Did the little urchin really just say that?

Jane continues, "I think it's really pretty."

Involuntarily my hand goes to my hair. Again I feel that facial twitch. But this feels different. Is this a smile? It is a most unfamiliar feeling.

"Well thank you, Jane," I stammer.

Jane pushes her glasses up on her nose and smiles. Plain Jane's face is transformed.

"Tomorrow," I say. "Tomorrow I'll bring that book."

Once again I think of that phrase that has haunted me all these years. "Those who can, do. And those who can't, teach." Maybe this is the child, maybe this is one that I can teach.

Oh WTF.

Jamie McNamara was born in and lived most of her life in various locations in New Jersey.

She graduated from William Paterson University with a BA in English after attending evening classes for years.

After spending weekends in upstate New York for 17 years, Jamie moved there in 2005. She lives in Unadilla and works in Oneonta, NY.

Jamie is a member of the HML Writers, a group sponsored by the Huntington Memorial Library in Oneonta, New York. She is working on writing short stories.

Paint It Blue
Beladee Nahem Griffiths

She wanted to paint her house blue. A deep indigo blue like the sky just before sunset. The kind of blue that is reaching into the dark depths of purple, but still not too far away from the blue of a beautiful sun-filled spring day. She would not paint the whole house blue. The upper half, where each shake shingle sat neatly one next to the other and each row below was staggered beneath the one above, would be blue. The lower half of her house she would paint white. Here, the horizontal clapboards stretched the length of the house and the two porches with their tall pillars and trellis work would all be white.

She felt the blue would show a happy house, a well-cared for house, a house an artist would like to brush a portrait of onto a clean piece of cream canvas. A lapis lazuli blue against the white would be fresh, bold, and joyful. The house was framed by her two yards, front and rear, and was surrounded by a white fence. The apple and cherry trees that bloomed in May, the bird bath frequented each day at noon by a flurry of sparrows, cardinals, robins, and her favorite the little black-capped chickadees, showed permanency and regularity. Whoever lived in such a house would be content with the hanging baskets spilling magenta petunias touched with splashes of white and purple and with vines trailing long and low from the beam of the front porch; such a house could not know heartache. The world would assume the inhabitant of such a house would not know any pain. As it stood, the house was green and white. Not an ordinary green, like the deep, dark green of an ancient cedar forest, nor a sickening, putrid green of sickness, or ill health. It was a curious yet soothing teal green with just enough blue in it to set her imagination free to fall into the deepest dreams of a blue that knew no sorrow.

She found herself standing before row upon row of paint samples, her mind reeling at the many shades of blue: from the blackest navy, to all the gradations of periwinkle, to white with only a tint of gray to still call itself blue. They had names like Sail Away, Midnight's Depth, or Ocean Voyage. Her eye went straight to the singular blue that remarkably rose from the depths of her center like an open flower born from the void. The healing blue rose like sapphire light from her heart through her throat, beyond her brow, and straight above the crown of her head. The blue hovered above her like a halo, like an aura, radiating and dazzling her. She took the two inch cardboard sample to the checkout desk and asked for five gallons. She carefully chose brushes, rollers, paint pans, gloves, and a tarp to place upon the ground. She bought a pair of white carpenter pants with pockets and loops to wear while she painted.

She waited for the first fine weekend. She awoke to sunshine and mild temperatures. She pulled out the sixteen-foot ladder from its resting place in the garage. She rolled and shook the paint can and pried the lid carefully off with a flat-head screwdriver. The liquid blue spilled into the paint pan like wine, like syrup, like something good enough to eat. She dipped her brush into the thickness of the paint, wiped off the excess at the edge and laid the first stroke of blue over the existing green. At first, she felt enormous disappointment. The two colors were so close she could not make out a difference, but after she finished the first long section, the blue seemed like the depths of the sea riding in waves against a white horizon and she was happy.

Perhaps, the blue was for water like the sea. Remembrance of waves wild and white-capped, with her sailboat skimming across them, the sun tipping each wave with a diamond until the whole sea sparkled and blinded her as she raced across its cerulean form. Perhaps, the blue covered the deep, dark green of the swollen river where her only daughter had capsized her kayak into the green of the spring rains. The swollen river, like her swollen belly in childbirth, had refused to give her up when she capsized into its churning, teal-green depths. The blue tried to fill the hole in her chest left by the loss of her beautiful, luminous girl. Her daughter that brought the sunshine in when she smiled and she was always smiling. The blue, the color of her eyes in the morning, when she woke from her sleepy dreams and saw her mother always there; always safe. The blue, like her energy when she bounded down the mat in gymnastics, and flew in circles around the uneven parallel bars to win trophies under the applause of the audience and her greatest admirer, her father. A rich indigo blue to cover the teal green that had sucked her sweet girl under the rolling waves to trap and steal her life away. The blue to cover the green that left her darling lying there, as if, in just the next moment, she would simply open her eyes. As if, in the next breath, she would sit up and smile her radiant smile once more. An indigo blue to remember her perfection and cover the green of her loss.

Beladee Nahem Griffiths is a teacher, artist, and writer. Raised in Brooklyn, she studied the violin, dance, and theater. Her drawings and paintings have appeared in gallery openings in Oneonta and Cooperstown, New York. Her writing has appeared in several anthologies in the region. She writes short stories, poetry, fiction, and creative nonfiction.

The Haunted House on Mulberry Street

Tricia Moore

It seemed to be the perfect night to visit the old, run-down house on Mulberry Street. It was a night of the new moon, dark and eerie. A storm was brewing on the horizon. Lightning flashed in the distance. Static electricity danced on the air.

"What are you waiting for?" Tommy asked Drew. "You lost the bet, now's the time to pay up."

"I'm going," Drew said back. He drew himself up tall. He knew that the others would tease him if he chickened out. Drew couldn't do that. He was one of the most popular kids in the school. The All-Star Athlete of Draper High. Drew had his reputation to uphold.

"Remember, if I do this," Drew turned to Tommy, "you have to squawk like a chicken in front of the assembly."

"Yeah, and if you chicken out, you will have those honors plus! I can hardly wait!"

By now a small group of the friends were standing around. They held their breath as Drew approached the house. One by one Drew walked up the rickety, creaking stairs. The wind moaned as it blew through the branches of the trees. The house groaned in response.

Drew reached for the door handle. He could hear his friends gasp as he opened the door. Giving them the high sign and a big, fake smile, he stepped inside. Behind him the door slammed shut. Fear grabbed him in the pit of his stomach. Chickening out, he grabbed the door handle, turned it and pulled. He pulled and pulled and pulled. The door wouldn't budge.

Drew sucked in a deep breath to calm his nerves. He wasn't going to let the stories of this place get to him. He knew there wasn't any such thing as ghosts. He'd never seen any. Besides, he had been in scarier places than this before. It didn't matter that he was alone. All alone!

Inside the house, all went quiet. Drew could hear his heart beating. Thump, thump, thump. He took a deep breath.

"There's no such thing as ghosts. There's no such thing as ghosts!"

"Are you sure?" a voice whispered in his ear.

"Aw!" he screamed. Running deeper into the house, he went. One room, then the next. He didn't slow down until he was in the kitchen area. Dishes were sitting in the drainboard. Pots and pans were on the stove, where they had been abandoned. Drew wondered why the people had taken off so quickly.

"Because they were afraid of me," a voice said, as if reading his mind.

This time Drew turned around, ready to confront this ghost.

"Leave me alone!" he shouted at the empty room. "You don't scare me."

"Are you sure?" the ghost asked.

"Yes!" Drew yelled.

"Why are you yelling at me?" the ghost asked. "I whispered in your ear. I didn't yell like this...." The ghost let out such an awful screech that the kids outside shook.

"Did you hear that?" Tommy asked the others.

The others stood there with their mouths wide open and nodded.

"I hope Drew is okay," Jill said nervously.

"If Drew was scared, he'd be out here," another boy said. "I wouldn't blame him. I wouldn't even go in. He's a hero."

The friends all nodded their heads.

Meanwhile, Drew was starting to think that this ghost wasn't so scary, after all.

"Who are you? Or, were you?" Drew asked, unsure of which was the proper way to speak to a ghost.

"I used to live here," he replied.

"What's your name?" Drew asked, again.

"Oscar," the ghost answered. "Thank you for asking."

"Why thank me?"

"Well, most people are afraid of me, like you were at first. I was a person, like you, many years ago."

"Why did you stay here?" curiously, Drew asked.

"Well, I built this house, back in 1831. It's my home."

"Wow!" Drew exclaimed. "That's a long time ago."

"I've seen a lot of people live in my house. Some were nicer than the others. Most took care of the place, so I stayed quiet," Oscar reminisced.

"What happened?" Drew asked.

"The last family that lived here weren't very respectful. They started to tear down a wall upstairs. I couldn't have that. There was nothing wrong with that wall."

"What did you do?"

"I howled, and howled. I blew cold air in their faces. Anything to get them to stop. I even hid their tools," Oscar grinned. "That was the most fun, hiding things from them. They would look high and low. Sometimes I'd return the things exactly where they had left them. Drove them nuts!" Oscar laughed and laughed. He laughed so hard that the house shook.

Outside some of Drew's friends screamed and ran. They weren't going to wait around for Drew. If he was crazy enough to stay in there, let him. Tommy tried to convince them to stay around.

"Don't leave. We told Drew we'd wait an hour for him to come out. What if he needs us?" Tommy shouted at the friends. Soon he and Jill were the only ones left.

"I'm staying," she said to Tommy. "If Drew is brave enough to go in there, then I'm brave enough to wait for him."

"Thanks," Tommy said to her.

Drew and Oscar soon became friends. (At least as much you can be friends with a ghost.) Oscar asked Drew if he'd like to see the whole house.

"Sure, if it's okay?" Drew told Oscar.

Oscar led Drew through the house, floor by floor. When they reached the attic, Drew was hesitant to go upstairs.

"What's wrong?" Oscar asked Drew.

"I don't like attics. They're scary," he replied.

Oscar laughed, "What's there to be afraid of? Ghosts?"

Realizing the reality of it Drew started to laugh, too. Soon both of them were laughing so hard that the house shook, again. From outside it sounded as if Drew was wailing in fright.

Tommy and Jill looked back and forth at each other.

"Do you think we should go inside and find him?" she asked Tommy.

"Let's wait to see if he yells again," Tommy answered.

"What if he's hurt?"

Looking at his watch, Drew saw how much time was left. With a sigh of relief he said, "Drew only has twenty minutes left. We should give it to him. If he isn't out by then, we'll go in." Jill agreed.

Up in the attic, Oscar had Drew removed an old floorboard, way over in a corner.

"I kept some stuff under there. I wanted to be remembered, hoping that someone like you would come along."

"Like me? Um, thank you for trusting me enough to see them."

"I'm so happy to share it with someone else. It's been so lonely around here. It's all I have left of my life and family," Oscar said, with a sad look on his face.

Drew thumbed through some pictures, one at a time, while Oscar told Drew stories about each one. He shared many memories.

Soon it was time for Drew to go. He explained to Oscar about the challenge he took.

"Want to scare your friends?" Oscar chuckled.

"Yeah, what did you have in mind?"

Drew and Oscar put their heads together and decided to wait until someone came in the house to find him.

A half hour went by. Tommy and Jill crept up the stairs. After they stepped inside, Drew came running down the stairs from the second floor, screaming and pulling at his hair. He ran right by them and out the door. The door seemed to slam behind him, of its own accord. Jill and Tommy froze. Oscar wailed. He made knocking sounds. In the kitchen he banged pots and pans together. Tommy was the first to scream.

Drew, laughing, came back inside. Tommy and Jill stared at him, as if he had lost his mind.

"Are you crazy?" Tommy shouted, "Let's get out of here!"

"Hold on," he said to them, "I have someone I'd like you to meet."

"Who's in here with you? You planned all this!" Tommy shouted at Drew.

Drew laughed, "Sort of. I want you to meet my new friend."

Oscar smiled. Drew had called him a friend. That warmed his ghostly heart.

"Oscar? Where are you?" he called out.

"I'm right here," Oscar whispered in his ear.

"Good, I want you to meet my friends. Will they be able to see you?" Drew asked.

Tommy saw Drew talking to thin air. Figuring he must have lost his mind, after all, staying in here so long, he told him they should go.

"Wait a minute. I want you to meet Oscar. He's the one who built this house. He lives here."

Tommy looked at Jill. Jill said, "Let's give him the benefit of the doubt."

Drew showed them into the living room and uncovered the sofa. They sat.

"Please, don't be scared," Drew told them. "Oscar is a little different."

Oscar started to materialize in front of them. They grabbed hands and squeezed.

When Oscar was able to be seen, Drew introduced him to his friends. They sat and stared.

"Pleased to make your acquaintance," Oscar said.

Jill was the first to speak. "Likewise."

Tommy nodded.

Drew told his friends all about the history of the house. Oscar felt comfortable enough to add to it. Before long the four of them were speaking, as if all was normal. An hour passed, then another. The kids soon realized that it was getting late and had to go home.

"We'll be back," Drew told Oscar.

Oscar thought Drew was just being nice. He was getting sadder by the minute. He started to wail softly, as he faded away.

"Oscar! Where did you go?" worried Drew asked.

"Oh, I'm right here," he whispered in Drew's ear.

"What's wrong?" Drew asked him, quietly.

"Well, I'm going to miss you. It's been real nice having someone to talk to. Don't forget me."

"Oscar, I won't forget you. I *promise* to come back. I'll bring some pictures of my family for you to see," Drew told him.

"Seriously?"

"Seriously. And I'm sure Tommy and Jill will come with me when they can," he told Oscar.

Tommy spoke up, "I promise to come back, too."

"Me, too," said Jill.

Oscar yelled with joy. All through the neighborhood, the people heard an awful sound come from the house. Looking out their windows, some of them saw the three children walking calmly from the house, with smiles on their faces.

Tricia lives in a small town in upstate NY with her husband, father, and two Jack Russells. She crosses genres in her fiction and writes children stories.

Run Away With Me
Rosa Quinones

In the early hours of the morning, Lola focused her attention on the exposed beams above her bed. The pain was excruciating and the nausea was not about to be ignored. She stood up slowly, feeling the cool hardwood floor under her feet. Looking towards the lavender trim of the bathroom door, she felt the bile hit the back of her throat. She made it to the edge of the bathtub before everything went white.

A deafening silence brought her out of unconsciousness. She heard the hum of the space heater outside the doorway and her morning alarm singing in the background. She lifted her arm to wipe her mouth, but shuddered at the sharp pain emanating from her back. Kidney pain wasn't new, but blacking out from it was.

Lifting her body from the bathroom floor sent throes through her veins, the motion of crawling only perpetuating the feeling. Lola managed to get to a phone. She melted to the floor, writhing in pain when she heard sirens.

The knock at the door was startling. The door swung open and in walked a rugged-looking bald man. He made his introductions in a thick Russian accent.

Lola already knew his partner's face, but she couldn't remember his name. He was the tall Italian-looking man that always seemed to catch Lola's eye around town. "Of course it would be him," she thought. The day she's flushed of her usual olive tone color, hair a mess and vomit on her breath, this handsome neighbor appears to save her. The Russian assessed her with questions. Feeling impatient and more uncomfortable than ever, Lola made her way to the ambulance, the Russian's arm keeping her steady.

It was a frigid New York morning. Far too cold to be outside in the pajamas Lola was wearing. Once the two men got Lola to the stretcher, the Russian moved to the driver's seat while Lola's neighborhood crush bundled her in blankets before starting an IV.

He hit a vein with ease despite the speeding ambulance.

"What can you give me for the pain?" Lola asked, trying to breathe evenly.

His emerald eyes met hers. "What do you want?" he asked, pulling out vials and rattling off names of drugs like it was cocktail hour.

Lola couldn't help but smile at the dry comedic relief and said, "Surprise me with something sweet."

"Comin' up," he said.

Lola began to feel the synthetic relief of the painkiller. She giggled at the jargon being used over the ambulance radio. The Italian smirked, knowing Lola was feeling the high. The Russian spoke up from the front seat, his accent struck Lola as hysterical. She started to laugh but was quickly halted by the rush of searing pain. It emanated from her back and up her torso. Soon everything went white again like the sun exploded before her.

Lola opened her eyes in a hospital bed that night. She heard Dr. Henderson speaking to a female figure on the other side of the curtain. "It's up to her now." Lola attempted to speak but her words were dashed by the familiar soreness of a dry, irritated throat. The doctor turned to see Lola's eyes wide with concern. She rushed over to Lola. Without finesse she told Lola, "This could have been avoided. The plan was simple." There was a pause as she shined a light in each of Lola's eyes. "I was leaving my shift when you came in. You're septic, Lola."

Everything the doctor said just blended together after that. From the beginning of her teenage years Lola was strongly advised to keep a water bottle close at hand. But like everything else in the recent months, her self-preservation felt less important. Depression seemed to manifest like a subconscious suicide. Her body rejected nourishment, making even the simplest tasks, like getting out of bed or putting on makeup, painstaking. The plan *was* simple...stay hydrated.

The thought of missing her flight over this was devastating. She needed to get home and finish packing.

"This could have been avoided." Lola swatted the echoing words away and wiped her tear-stained face. An RN came bouncing into the room. Apparently, the whole ward could hear Lola's anxiety, the screaming heart monitor calling attention to her increasing heart rate. The delicate-looking blonde asked Lola if she was in pain. Lola shook her head no, still trying to compose herself.

Dr. Henderson reappeared early the next morning. She knew Lola wasn't going to sit much longer. Luckily for Lola, Dr. Henderson wasn't one to waste time. She felt very strongly that her patients could heal better when they were comfortable in their own home.

"As long as your blood and urine samples come back normal, you're going home, Lola. You'll be on a high dose of antibiotics for at least 10 days and I want a follow up in two weeks." Lola knew she wouldn't be there in two weeks, but she agreed anyway.

Afternoon fell and Lola's IV was unhooked and her blood drawn, before she was carefully escorted to pee in a cup. She was relieved to see her urine no longer resembled mud. When the doctor came back to read Lola her results, administration followed with discharge papers and instruction.

"I'm sending you home on 500mg of antibiotics twice-daily with food and hydrocodone for the pain as needed. Fix this Lola," she warned before walking out of the room. Lola nodded in understanding.

In the days to follow, she would cling to her water bottle, eat well and vegetate in her bed as directed. She would fix this.

• • • •

LOLA DANCED THROUGH a haze of smoke, her silhouette fluttering against the light of the Cheyenne lamp her father bought her when she was eight. She moved with caution, her motions slight yet full of intent. A dance and a smoke to celebrate the freedom from pain and a fully packed suitcase. The restlessness that seemed to be constantly rattling in her chest was momentarily at ease knowing she would make her flight. Lola always did spontaneous things, but never like this. She was going to experience adulthood the way she had always imagined it.

• • • •

THE CARIBBEAN HEAT hit like a wall as the airport doors led Lola to her next home. Old San Juan was a dream to Lola's old soul. She had visited as a teenager with family that once called the island home. She could now call PR home too. A cab dropped her off on Calle San Francisco where Lola had rented a spacious studio above a vintage shop. Lola became well acquainted with the shop owner Frankie and his partner Ramón when she reserved many pieces to furnish her new digs. Lola spent the next three days sipping Bustelo on her balcony, walking around her new neighborhood and perfecting her beginner Spanish phrases on the locals.

Lola spent her first weekend in paradise working. She had been hired as a bartender at a local watering hole: a beautiful outdoor bar with large umbrellas over every table and lights strung between the two brick walls above the blue cobblestone alleyway.

Luckily for Lola, the bar owner's wife Silva was a distant relative by marriage who owed her uncle a favor. Silva reassured her not be too concerned about the language barrier. "A pretty half-breed like you will do fine! Just smile real pretty. No one will notice how bad your Spanish is m'ija. Most everyone is bilingual anyway."

Some time spent in the sun, a little red lipstick and Lola could almost blend. When customers ordered their poison in Spanish, Lola would smile real pretty, say, "I'm sorry?" and hope they would repeat themselves in English. If that failed, her male counterpart Miguel usually came to her rescue. The two ran a smooth operation and their tips reflected so.

Miguel had been raised on the island and was every bit the gentleman Puerto Rican mothers pride themselves on raising. Always opening doors and insisting on walking Lola home, even fending off the occasional drunk who thought he might have a shot at Lola.

Of course she fantasized about them falling madly in love, planning a beach wedding and making beautiful tan babies together. Miguel was handsome and generous but Lola kept him at arm's length. Always thanking him for the walk home, but never waiting too long before walking upstairs. Lola was enjoying her new freedom. She ate well, took salsa lessons, read on the beach. She even worked in the shop with Frankie and Ramón from time to time. Lola had been enjoying herself. Life was calm in a way she had never known.

Hurricane Maria put an end to that calm. The cobblestone streets were littered with turmoil. Lola's building had been spared, but Silva's bar didn't fare so well. With no work and no resources in sight, Lola tried to focus her energy on caring for those nearest her. With what few resources did become available in the coming days, Lola would find, gather and distribute goods to some of the elderly in her building. She went looking to enlist Miguel in helping Frankie and Ramón clear debris from the street in front of the shop, only to find he was among the missing. A family member staying at his apartment waiting for his return delivered the news to Lola. Hearing this, she put her hand to her chest in fear her heart might hit the pavement. She joined search parties and continued to gather and distribute goods with fellow neighbors. What else could she possibly do with so much suffering surrounding her? Supplies were short everywhere and it was especially hard to come by clean water. Lola exhausted herself daily with little to no hydration.

Once again, she found herself on the bathroom floor with a familiar pain tugging at her side. Lola managed to find her voice long enough to call out the open window for Frankie and Ramón. They both came running.

Without doctors or pain meds available, all Lola could hope for was water. Frankie and Ramón rallied a few other shop owners and found Lola two gallon jugs of water. Over the next seven days, the two jugs were finished. By some miracle, Lola's pain subsided. After spending the majority of the week in bed, Lola began to regain strength. She had volunteered for a search party that afternoon in hopes of finding Miguel.

She reached for the Cheyenne lamp on her bedside table. Still no juice. She drew the curtains to let in the harsh Caribbean sunlight and opened her balcony doors. The narrow streets of Old San Juan were quiet, except for Frankie and Ramón competing in a lover's spat on their stoop below her. Lola made her morning coffee and stepped out onto her balcony. Her eyes adjusted to the light and she noticed there was a lineman atop almost every electrical pole lining the street. She then realized the loud male voices she had heard weren't Frankie's and Ramón's at all. The linemen were singing what almost sounded like a military cadence. Their voices sounded deep and strong – almost determined. Neighbors and shop owners started poking their heads out to listen. Lola sipped her coffee and listened in amazement. It was the perfect stolen moment to pull hope from. Lola finished her coffee, feeling renewed. She got dressed in clothes that hadn't been washed for weeks and made her way to the site the search party was covering. The area had been flattened by the storm. Much of Miguel's family had joined the search party. The site was in the same neighborhood where Miguel's best friend from childhood had been living.

Not a soul was found that day. The feeling of hope Lola had felt while listening to the linemen only hours ago had been crushed by the reality that Miguel might never be found. When night fell, Lola knew there was no chance of sleep. She lay in bed searching for a new place of calm.

In weeks to come, power still had not been completely restored, but food and water were easier to come by. Lola had given all of herself to the effort of rebuilding the paradise around her.

As a thank-you for all their support and love, Lola worked a full day in the shop with Frankie and Ramón, getting things ready for the reopening. At the end of the day, she went upstairs and enjoyed a Malta on her balcony. Most nights, sleep still eluded her, but tonight she wasn't worried about it. She could sleep on the plane in the morning.

Rosa Quinones had an enlightening year of travel in 2017, which lead into a deep passion for writing. Experiencing new people and places nationwide was the perfect muse to begin this excursion.

Rosa is currently working in healthcare as a CNA, and is looking to further improve her education, whilst enjoying everything life has to offer.

Strawberry Tigers
Angelika Mahnert

In an old house on Strawberry Hill there lived a woman, whose son had traveled many a times to India. He had become an expert on the wildlife of the subcontinent and was very interested in the preservation of tigers there.

One night the woman had a dream. She found herself walking in the meadows of Strawberry Hill with her son as they often love to do, only that it was in the middle of the night.

Heading towards the bottom of the hill, where a river runs, they found themselves enchanted as always when they arrived there and continued to stroll towards the bend of the river, where a thin rim of woods shelters the riverbed. In a still and deep spot the water lay quietly and showed a perfect reflection of the full moon. The stars were the brightest ever and the moon-light threw large moon-shadows of the trees onto the fields, which it had covered with silver.

Mother and son ducked down into the dark shadows of an immense old oak-tree and waited. It was a mild wonderful night in late spring and they could hear the waters of the river flow in a lively spring-rush while all else seemed quiet.

But there, only about two arms-lengths away, the grasses part and the outlines of two large cats appear.

The two humans under the oak-tree hold their breath: this is the moment they had wished for! The Strawberry-Tigers were out for a prowl! How lucky it was to encounter them tonight, because to actually see them is an absolutely rare event...As the two first tigers crouch down in front of the stunned onlookers, a third one slides through the underbrush towards them. They have discovered a patch of strawberries and begin to feast on them. Stunning how BIG these creatures are so close up! All three are too busy munching strawberries to even notice their observers.

"Hatchou!" the woman suddenly had to sneeze. Six yellow eyes peek at her and her son, who both still tuck in the shadow of the old oak-tree. For an instant a flash of clear and present danger rises in the mother's heart remembering the tigers of India, who one would not wish to surprise this way!

But the Strawberry-Tigers know better: they don't need to fear us. They continue to purr and munch on the fragrant red fruit in the grass as mother and son now feel invited to join them at the tiger-feast: how unspeakably DELICIOUS! What an amazing THRILL!

Oh, beautiful stars and moon and sweet strawberries and tame, vegetarian tigers!!! The woman let herself lean against one of the huge striped cats feeling its soft fur and smelling strawberry-breath all around her.

What a place! What a world! Taste it right now!

Tiger-berries, Tiger-moon

the dream is over all too soon

Sudden Red out of the Blue
Angelika Mahnert

The neighbors were building their new house. It sat on a hill behind the weekenders' garden.

The weekenders were grandpa and grandma, who brought their young grand-daughter often to that special place in the green. They cherished the flower-strewn meadow topped by a stand of white birches. Out of the city into the emerald sway of grasses waving in the breeze, aspen-leaves rustling and a multitude of birds with their varied songs and calls enlivening the carefree hours spent on that hill.

They had named it "Frederick's Height", where Grandpa Frederick sat gazing over stretches of rolling hillsides from his favorite perch.

This time their peace was somewhat disrupted by the incessant banging of a hammer from behind the bushes and trees dividing their property from their neighbors'. Their neighbor, Mr. Horvath, was on his tall ladder to install gutters on his almost-finished home. The weekenders knew how proud and excited he felt having built this house by himself with only the help of his strong and capable wife, of whom he was proud as well. Autumn would be arriving in the span of a few weeks. Leaves and rain would fall, gutters had to function. The Horvaths wished to have all the outside work completed come winter. They also dreamed to be able move in before the cold season.

While the grandfather sat as usual on his favorite lawn-chair under the birches reading the weekend-papers and grandma picked berries to take back home to make some fine pie, the grand-daughter rocked on a swing tied to a sturdy tree-branch. There she could rock and swing the hours away, in the lovely freshness of the country-air brushing against her young face and swing-pumping legs pushing herself off the ground with happily-bare feet.

Then out of the blue a dull, but loud thump- then the neighbor's wife's scream. The girl jumped off her swing- startled and curious. What had happened?

The bushes at the edge of the two properties were thick. Hawthorn, brambles and dense Honeysuckle grew there. The little girl ducked under those branches. She heard the neighbor's wife talking hastily on the phone before she saw anything. Pushing the branches aside she felt breathless and somewhat panicked. The voice on the phone caught on to her. It got under her skin.

Before she could do much, but scramble closer, there was already an ambulance. Now the girl watched two men emerging from the white van with the red cross. Next they carried Mr. Horvath on a stretcher, a heavy-set man with a thick head covered with short, stubbly, black hair and Mrs. Horvath running along the two ambulance-men veiling and helplessly flailing her arms. The last the girl could witness was red blood streaming from both of Mr. Horvath's ears as he raised his torso up as in protest before he was lifted into the dark rear of the van.

Angelika Mahnert grew up in the city of Graz in Austria, Europe. Her father was a physician, her mother a classical singer. After receiving a Masters of Pharmacy degree at the University of Graz and the completion of the apothecary year and exam, she married a young American physician and followed her husband to the United States.

Writing seemed always innate to her. She vividly remembers when a poem about elves by a forest-pond, which she had lovingly illustrated, had been confiscated in Elementary School study hall. One of her favorite things in High School was writing essays.

In 2008- after the children left home, she moved from Connecticut to Cooperstown. In 2011 she was thrilled to discover the Smithy Writers' Circle brought to life by Danielle Newell (Henrici).

In 2014 "The Wordsmiths" published an anthology.

Now a member of the Huntington Memorial Library writers' group, she enjoys meeting on Saturdays in Oneonta. It is a much larger group with an interesting array of writers and writing styles. It is often inspiring to hear the varied and diverse results. The welcoming and supportive environment of HML Writers encourages and offers a sense of camaraderie helping to balance the otherwise more solitary occupation of writing.

The Wyrm of DuFacies

P. A. Curran

Mr. Ferguson got our attention by whispering one word, "Ghosts". At that word, everyone moved forward as I moved back. I'm not really interested in that stuff, not that it scares me, just not interested. The shaking of my hands was probably because I was dehydrated. I needed water.

Mr. Ferguson had been telling us the history of the library, how it was a house, and some rich guy named DuFacies donated it with a special request, that it be used as a library and only a library. He even specified the hours of operation, seemed like a control freak.

But while a few were mildly interested in the history, the others in my eighth-grade class were bored. Come on I'm 12, having story time in the library made no sense. I preferred the silent enjoyment of reading, alone. Mom would typically find me wriggled into a corner, with not one but several books scattered about.

Plus, the guy was distracting. He had no hair on his head, tufts of grey hair coming out of places that shouldn't be, his ears, and ew, his nose. He was probably 90. The most disturbing thing about Mr. Ferguson was his dark, bushy eyebrows. They seemed to have a life of their own, waving at you as he read. He was sitting in a great leather chair reading, a big cup of tea or coffee balanced on the arm, that somehow never fell off.

Mr. Ferguson looked over at Ms. O'Brien, my eighth-grade teacher. She was sitting in the Sun, what little there was at this hour, her face tracking it across the sky like a sunflower. She was old too, not Ferguson old, but maybe 40. She was also rail thin and moved slowly. I watched as she leaned forward, closing her eyes. I should have noticed when coming to the library something was wrong with her. We had to stop a few times for her to catch her breath, which was weird, she would usually set a pace that made all of us sweat by the time we arrived.

In a whisper, he continued, "There's not one but several who prowl the halls at night. Floating here and there, and do you know what they are doing?"

Most shook their heads side to side, but Stanley chimed in and said, "They are looking for a spooooky book." This got a chuckle out of a few kids, and Stanley sat up straighter. He liked attention, he also liked intimidating people. He wasn't the brightest or biggest, just the meanest and something we all had to deal with.

Mr. Ferguson looked at Stanley, the chuckles died down and he kept staring at him. It was unnerving, Stanley tried returning the stare, but Mr. Ferguson was in a league of his own and it didn't take long for Stanley to look down.

Clearing his throat, Mr. Ferguson continued, "They are patrolling the Library, ensuring that no one comes and removes the books, because they are special, as I'm sure your teachers have said, knowledge is power! They are in-charge of making sure that the books and tomes are all in order," leaning back he smiled, "And some light dusting now and then."

That got everyone to laugh. Ms. O'Brien turned to see Mr. Ferguson looking at her. She smiled, "We're done already? Well the time sure flies." She said as she got up with a grimace. "Kids" she said with a clap, "let's gather our things and thank Mr. Ferguson." I turned with the others saying thank you.

I decided to head to the bathroom before we left, that's where the water fountain is, you know because I was dehydrated. As I walked by Mr. Ferguson, a book fell out of his tattered sports coat. I bent down to pick it up and as soon as I touched it, my hand and arm felt tingly. Like when you sleep on top of your hand, then you roll over, you feel tiny pins and needles stabbing you.

Up close, I could tell it was old and smelled funky, like sour milk left in a cup for a few days. The cover was leather with some strange writing on it. As I brought it up, Mr. Ferguson turned and saw me with the book. His face became as red as an over ripe tomato ready to burst. Stuttering, spittle flying from his lips, he reached out, his fingers hooked into claws ready to tear me apart and he screamed "THIEF!" ripping the book out of my hand, knocking his cup off the arm of the chair. I started shaking, shocked at what just happened. Mr. Ferguson stormed out, muttering to himself about a thief taking his stuff. That's when Stanley and his crew, pointed over at me laughing. I then noticed my pants were wet in an awkward spot.

I left quickly to the restroom, my hands shaking. I had seen that look before, well the emotions behind it. My shaking got worse, as I thought of my dad. I had grabbed his work backpack, it was partially opened. Dad's face was the same as Mr. Ferguson's, when he grabbed it from me. I knew it wasn't from anger, but something else. Something that made the shakes happen, it was not anger but fear, fear in his eyes. That same fear I just saw in Mr. Ferguson.

I cleaned up in the bathroom. Mr. Ferguson prefers tea. That was good cause it shouldn't stain my pants, I didn't have many. I found a comfortable stall and pulled my legs up, they are longer than most. I'm tall but going through that awkward phase where my arms and legs just are not listening to me.

I did it with a comfortable practice, I had been in this position before. I closed my eyes. It was the end of the school day and I would just have to wait about 15 mins for Stanley and his crew to clear out.

When I woke up, my legs were asleep. I slowly lowered them and looked at my hand, the one that touched the book. It felt fine, there was a smudge like ink from a newspaper. I rubbed my legs down, the lights were off. Damn, I must have dozed off.

Legs stiff, I pushed the stall door open and shuffled over to the sink to wash my face. My blonde hair was all a mess. Using some water, I tried to straighten any of it, and gave up. I knew it was late but wasn't worried. Mom was working her second, or maybe third shift tonight so she wouldn't be home. I'd have to grab something to eat as I walked home. Looking human once again, I opened the door to leave.

I noticed the lights were different, on but somehow muted. I shuffled down the row of books and saw a lady looking over a title then placing it back on the shelf. Huh, costume night I thought. The lady was wearing a complicated get-up, with a lot of skirts and her hair up in a tight bun. She was wearing a fluffy shirt, no ladies wear blouses, it was white, and frilly. She turned away from me and quickly went down the row of books, without slowing she just slammed in-to the wall.

Well, that's what should have happened. If I tried doing that, I would have a bloody nose at least. But the lady just kept walking, and entered, passed, phased I have no idea what she did except walk thru the wall. Shuffling slowly, I went to the wall, my hands shaking a bit, I touched the where the librarian had been. It was solid. I tried pushing, even slapping it, nothing. It was real, a real wall.

The story about the library, well what I had thought was a story Mr. Fergu-son had told earlier came to mind. I noticed it was harder to breath, as the shaking progressed from my hands to my stomach, I was sure to be sick. I pushed away from the wall and went down another aisle of books looking for the exit.

There in another row was a girl about my age. She was dressed in a leather jacket, too big for her. Her hair was sticking up in places, I think that was on purpose because while most of her hair was dark, almost black, the clumps sticking up were different colors, red, yellow, orange, and purple. Black leggings went down to a pair of black converse sneakers. I only saw part of her profile; the bottom of her ear was filled with earrings.

Another ghost. Shaking, I held my breath, but didn't do a good job. The girl turned, she had a ring in her nose, and bright blue, no her eyes were green. She turned, then punched me in the nose, knocking me down on the floor. "Ow, what was that for!"

"That heavy breathing thing you were doing was creepy "she said, then turned back to the book in her hand.

Well, not a ghost. "Ah, Sorry?" I tried as I got up.

She snorted and blew some hair out of her face then turned to face me, book in her hand. "Yeah, well don't get any ideas."

Hands up, I said, "Sure, sure no problem. Can you just tell me how to get out of here, I'm a little turned around, I need to get out of the library but can't seem to find the door I used this afternoon."

Her eyes got big then, she dropped the book she had in her hands, then leaned toward me, close. I felt a little weird as her face pressed close to mine, then quickly, she bent down and licked my neck. It was quick, her tongue was rough and cool against my skin. She leaned back, eyes wide. "Stay here," she said, then without taking her eyes off me she backed out of the book aisle looking around. Her lips parted, almost in a grimace that showed way too many teeth, pointy and small.

That's when I finally looked around. The metal bookcases were no longer there, they were replaced by ones made from some dark wood. I turned to the shelves and even the books were different, while they were still books, they were no longer the titles I expected. Instead of Harry Potter, and books by Stephen King, there were titles like, WereWolves, Thar Wolves, by Jennifer O'Hue, Which, Witch are you, let's Find Out!, and Things that go Bump in the night, and why we need to unionize!

I bent down and picked up the book that the not-ghost girl dropped. My hand tingled a little as I picked it up and turned it over, the cover said, Lineage and history of Us.

Weird, no idea what that meant. I looked up as the not-ghost girl was coming back with a boy. He might be a little older, his skin was dark, and his hair was blonde, but the kind you get from a bottle not nature. He leaned forward, I stepped back, while the lick from the girl was OK, I was not interested in being licked from him. But he was quicker than me. Though he looked scrawny, his hands were strong and held me in place, he leaned in and sniffed.

He let go, as I rubbed my arms where he had grabbed me. He turned to, not-ghost girl, and said, "Margo, I can smell it on him." Ah not-ghost girl is Margo. When he said her name, it was more like MARRRGO, there were so many rolling Rs I'm not sure how to write it down.

He wrapped one arm around his waist, then propped his other, up and stroked his upper lip, "Hmm do you have your card?" He said, again the rolling RRRs.

"Sure," I said, showing him my library card.

He bent to take a closer look, then started shaking his head. To Margo he said, "This is strange. Margo, I think we should stay away from him. The Librarian will be making her rounds. Once she realizes he should not be here, she will not be happy. She's been in such a mood, I'm not sure what she may do."

Margo, her eyes still wide and staring at me, shook her head. Turning she said, "Maybe a good idea Carlos, we need to stay away from the Norman. By the way, the mustache is coming in nicely."

Carlo smiled, a big beaming smile which would have comforted me if his teeth weren't so big. Again, what is up with all the teeth.

Margo looked at me again, eyes back to blue, "Do you know where you are?" she asked, in that voice you use when speaking to little children, who are confused, or you think will cry if you scare them.

Rolling my eyes, I said "Duh, the library."

Margo looked at Carlos, then back at me shaking her head. At the same time, they both said, "The Duo Facies Bibliotheca, The Two face Library." Then Margo continued, waving a hand around to the bookcases, "Look around, didn't you notice how different this is. These are not normal books, special ones that only those in the supernatural community know exist. You are not super-natural, you shouldn't be here. You're going to be in big trouble."

I looked around, down at the end of the aisle, something passed by, a book in its hands, no paws, they were covered in fur with long sharp claws. It was wearing a hoodie, so I couldn't see it's face, but I knew for sure the music com-ing out of the Beats headphones was Coldplay.

This was too much. I felt my fear rising, I needed to get out of here. "I'll leave right now," I told them both. "Thanks, I can find my way out" I said, as I put the book Margo had dropped back on the shelf.

As the book touched the shelf, both sucked in air. I turned to look at them, staring at me. Looking past them, I saw the older woman, she must be the Li-brarian. Her face was stern, but I saw what I didn't before; I saw her, but it was like looking at something through the haze of a hot summer day. She shim-mered and wiggled in places.

She didn't pass through but walked around Carlos and Margo and came straight at me. Standing in front, she calmly looked down at the book I held, then turned slowly, my eyes following her gaze to a small card on the book case. In fancy handwriting, the little card stated, Please do not re-shelve the books. Thank you, the Librarian.

She then turned slowly, back to me, me who had a hand on a book that I was in the process of shelving. She reached out, and I placed the book her hand. Her little finger brushed against my hand and she hissed, it sounded like the sucked in air Carlos and Margo had taken was now escaping from her.

She turned, looked at the spine of the book, then looking at me again, placed it on the shelf. I couldn't help but notice she was placing it exactly where I was going too.

Eyes on me again, they were cloudy, no way she could see, but as she looked at me there was no doubt that she saw me.

The Librarian pointed to the door leaving the Library, which just happened to have been a wall not a minute ago. Happy to oblige, I turned quickly walking as fast as I could to the door. Looking behind me, I saw her turn to Carlos and Margo, her hand out, palm up. As the door closed behind me, I heard, Margo begin to sob.

Once out into the night air, I took a deep breath. The whole time with the Librarian, I had held it in, not even realizing it. I should have turned and ran home then, but didn't. I sat on the stairs and waited. Carlos walked out, his arm around Margo who was crying into her hands. Carlos guided her to the steps of the library, where they both sat.

I moved closer to them, Margo didn't look up, just hissed, like the neighbor's cat when you catch him by surprise. Anger was in her voice as she said, "Get away from me. This is your fault, my one chance to findoooouuut..." she couldn't finish as she cried.

Carlos patted her back as he turned to me. "I am sorry, she, well the Library was very important for her, ah research." He said the word, but it wasn't just a word there was a weight a heaviness to it that said there was more to it. I remembered the book Margo had, Lineage and History of Us.

"I'm sorry. I fell asleep, I didn't mean to cause this problem," I said.

"Well you did," Margo whispered again, her face still hidden by her hands. "My one chance, my chance to find, find out who, what I am, is now gone. Lost because of you." she said the last, as she put her hands down by her side, eyes, green again, boring into me. I flinched back from that stare. If Carlos wasn't there, I wasn't sure I would make it home.

Carlos explained that you had to have a Library card to access the Library. Without those cards, you were unable to enter the Library at night. I looked to Carlos; his tanned face was wet, not from Margo but his own tears. "You see," he started, sighed then began again, "I know who and what I am. I'm a werewolf, as my father, mother and brothers are. But I'm different, I, this is difficult to say, I'm a pescatarian. Well at least I want to be."

Shaking my head and seeing my chance to possibly bond with Carlos, I said "I am too. I was born on March 11th, you?" Carlos shaking his head, spoke slowly, like you would to a young child. I was getting really annoyed at the way they were both treating me. "No, no, a P-E-S-C-A-T-A-R-I-A-N is a vegetarian that also eats fish. Not one born in the cycle of the fish. I need the Library to show my parents that another Were also took a different path."

Sighing, and rubbing his hands together Carlos looked at Margo then me. I could tell he was nervous, unsure if he wanted to share. Then he started. "You see my kind, we are big meat eaters. We're hunters, we prefer to eat what we hunt." Looking down at his feet, almost like he was embarrassed, he continued, "What we kill."

Carlos' cheeks became wet. Still looking down he said, "You see, I am close to my time to change. At the next full moon, my family expects me to change with them and run, and hunt. To track something, run it down with the pack, scaring it, and with it in that frightened state, sink our teeth into it, tearing and rending the flesh. Spraying each other in it's warm blood..." Carlo paused, and I noticed he couldn't continue. Hesitant at first, I sat down next to him and patted him on the back, trying to help comfort him. Carlos, moved so fast he was a blur, wrapping his arms around my waist, burying his head into my shoulder he released his pain. Crying on me was awkward, but I could deal with that, it was screaming, that really caught me off guard. He was loud. I looked around, checking to see if anyone was rushing to help, thinking he was attacking me, sadly no. Just snot, tears and more snot making my shirt wet. I'd need a new one.

I could tell the honesty from Carlos caught Margo by surprise. She stood up, looking at both of us, wiping away her tears, then bent down and wrapped her arms around us, yelling "Group hug!"

We snickered at first, not quite laughing out loud. Carlos leaned back, looked at each of us with anger. Then he let out a full belly laugh that got Margo and I going again so we all laughed out loud.

Carlos, calming down, looked back to Margo, "I'm sure we will gain access again, just give it time. The Librarian is just mad and frustrated right now."

I looked at them and asked, "What happened? Also, Hi, my name is Thomas. Why did you call me Norman before?"

Carlos and Margo laughed, introducing themselves, Margo answered, "Normans and Normas are our name for, well people like you. You're well normal, non-supernatural people."

Carlos leaned forward and continued, "This library changes. At night, the supernatural Library comes to this place, time, dimension. I'm not sure where it goes during the day. It is a place that allows us to conduct research, and we'll feel safe. Much of our history has been lost, simply because no one ever considered putting the information of us into one place."

"How did you find out about the Library? Are you part of a secret club?"

Margo, rolling her eyes, said "Hello, there is something called The Internet? You just need to know what to look for."

Carlos shrugged his shoulders saying, "My parents told me. But you, I've never thought it was possible, a Norman entering our Library!"

"Well, I didn't really enter. I was there before they closed," I said, a little embarrassed and not ready to admit I had been hiding in the bathroom.

Margo turned to me. Her eyes blue again. "Yes, but again, you were in the library, which would have shifted, phased, whatever it does. You, well you just shouldn't have been there or even able to enter the Library."

Carlos picked up, "When we first got our library card, it was explained to us that there are wards about the Library. Normans can't see it, let alone enter. Look at it, what do you see?"

I looked and said "Well, it's the library. The windows dark, no lights on."

Carlos turned to Margo, "And you my dear, what do you see?"

Margo replied, "I see the building, as what I assume it looks like during the day-time. But when I look from the side, out of the corner of my eye, there is a haze to it, it shimmers, almost like it's not really here."

"Exactly!" Carlos said. "That is the protections you are seeing. We could go right up there, and the door would open for us. Well, that is if we had our cards."

I was looking at the Library from the side, like Margo had done. I thought maybe I could almost make something. I said "I am really sorry. Sorry for the pain and trouble I caused. I wish there was something I could do. But," my shoulders went up in a shrug.

Carlos shook his head, "I know you are sorry, I accept your apology. It's not your fault. The Librarian has been on edge ever since the book went missing."

"Book?" I asked.

"Yes,", Carlos said sitting down next to Margo, "The Library's books are special and can only be taken out with a library card. But some are never allowed to leave. They are available for research, but the wards would stop you from removing a special book. So, no one knows how, but the book is just not here anymore."

"What, why? A library that has books but that you cannot check them out? That makes no sense," I said.

Margo looking up at me with her tear streaked eyes, made me wipe mine. Dust or something got in them and blurred my vision as she said, "Most books can be checked out of the Library. But as Carlos said, some are special, powerful, and power like that is not allowed to leave. Only a few can read them, and you cannot remove them, just not possible."

"The Librarian has taken it personally.", Carlos continued, "Because it is her responsibility to keep the books in order. She has been out of sorts ever since."

Margo, wiping the remaining tears from her eyes, smearing her black make-up even more on her face to make her look, well zombie-ish, said, "I know it wasn't on purpose. I also accept your apology."

I rubbed my fingers, "I don't know how you guys can pick up those books, just the one gave me a shock."

They both looked at me, their eyes said it all, they had no idea what I was talking about. Rubbing my hand, I said, "You know a tingling on the hand, you don't get that when you picked up those books?"

Both shook their heads side to side. "Well I said, at least it wasn't like the..." I stopped, I swear you could hear the gears in my head spin, then click, as it all slipped into place. A smile spread on my face as I turned and said to Carlos and Margo, "I have a plan. We need to meet here tomorrow. At the library, the Norman's library after school. Do you go to school? But ah," I stammered not sure if I should mention the next part, "Can you, you know come out during the day. You don't burst into flames or, well twinkle in the daylight or something weird like that?"

They both laughed. "I go to John Jay Middle School," Margo said.

Carlos, shaking his head, said "I can stand in the light, I'm just a were. We'll meet you here tomorrow, after school." I wanted to ask, but we were getting along, and well I didn't want to ruin the moment.

It was the longest school day of my life. It felt like the seconds were minutes and the minutes were hours. Even though it took forever, I have no idea what happened. I floated from one class to the other, not paying attention. I somehow even missed Stanley and his antics.

After school I ran to the library. I was there outside before the others, waiting quietly on the steps. I wondered if they would ask if I had trouble getting home so late. I was trying to help them, but there were still things I wouldn't talk about. Having your mom work two full jobs and never seeing her 'cause your dad isn't around was a topic I didn't want to discuss

A young girl sat down next to me. I turned smiling, then blurted, "You!"

It was Margo. Gone was the leather, the earrings, and strangely the multi-colored hair. Her hair was dark, long and curly. She looked, well looked like someone I would want to know.

She punched me in the arm, playfully this time. "Quit staring, creeper." she said, a smile playing on her lips. I looked away, realizing she was right, I was staring. "I know," she sighed, then continued. "I feel weird like this. Like I'm wearing a costume. Well, I am during the day. It's weird that I can only really be me at night."

"I'm sorry, but I know that's not going to help. It never helped me," I said quickly, the words left me before I could stop them. She turned and smiled at me. A wonderful smile, her teeth were small, pointy. A reminder that she was different. I smiled, feeling good. I leaned back saying, "So, where is he, do you think he bailed?"

"Nah, he had practice. Should be here soon." Margo said. Then from around the corner Carlos strolled, in full soccer regalia. Shorts, knee length socks and his school's jersey. Cleats slung over his shoulder, he looked picture perfect, confident. I wondered if he was any good, knowing he was.

"Sorry, Margo and Thomas," he said, again with about a million RRRs tumbling out of his mouth. "Varsity just finished."

I noticed how he dropped that, like no one would notice, "Varsity". Yeah, he was barely in High School, yet he played on the varsity team, of course he did. I realized I disliked him a little for that. No real reason, I don't even play soccer, sorry Futbol. But it wasn't jealousy I mean why would I be jealous of his rolling RRRs, almost not quite dead caterpillar of a mustache and being on a team. A team that accepted him. Yeah, no jealousy at all.

Margo got up turning to me, "Tom, this was your idea, why are we here?"

I stood up, my hands surprisingly sweaty, what if I was wrong? What if I got them here and they found out I wasn't sure, they would be mad, pissed. Probably never talk to me again, which would be OK because they weren't like me, a Norman. I'm sure they talked about me behind my back. Probably laughed all night... oops, they were staring at me.

Clearing my throat, "Ah, well I have an idea about where the book, the one the Librarian is looking for, well at least who had it last. I'm sure it's still with him. It's in there with Mr. Ferguson." I said, pointing to the library.

Margo sat down like all her bones had turned to jelly. Carlos looked at me shocked, then shaking his head said, "No, no simple Thomas, that is just not possible," Carlos said as he moved to Margo, putting his arm around her. "The Library is not like your library. Yours allows anyone to come in with a card and take books away. As we said this book was special, and not allowed to leave."

Margo sighed, got up shaking her head, "For a minute, I thought there was a chance. I'm out." she said and started walking down the hill.

"Margo, please wait, it's in there I know it is. Please, I..." but she didn't listen to me and continued down the hill.

I turned to see Carlos looking, noticing he had intense blue eyes. Finally, he shook his head up and down quickly, then said, "It can't be there, but I see that you believe it is. I need this, I will be of age soon and need to have an answer or I will have to start hunting and even," he shook as he said the last word, "kill." He made a retching sound at the last part. He continued "But I see that you believe, and I believe that you believe, so perhaps that is enough. I will go with you." I looked back, toward where Margo went, then shook my shoulders and said, "Well, come on then." He reached up and clapped me strongly on the shoulder, "Let us find a Fer Gus An."

"Ah, I said, Mr. Ferguson is a name, well the name of the guy who reads stories to us." Carlos reached up and tousled my hair. "Ah, you still like to be read to. I liked that too, when I was a baby," he said walking past me into the library, yes I really disliked him.

We found him quickly, on the first floor in the kids' book section. He was reading Jack and the Beanstalk to a bunch of rugrats, all sitting at his feet, not moving, just staring at him. Weird, I mean they were little kids, yet no one was itching, twitching or moving at all.

All the kids were staring at Mr. Ferguson wearing his tattered sports coat. I turned to Carlos, only to find that he had sank down onto the floor, listening to Mr. Ferguson. No not listening, entranced by him. I grabbed Carlos by the arm and half dragging half lifting took him out of the room.

Carlos shook his head, and was confused for a minute, then looking around he said, "Thomas. I understand why you listen to him reading. His voice drew me in, it was like I was there, climbing the beanstalk with Jack. I swear I saw the other kids too. How is that possible?"

"The book," I said. "It changed something about him."

Shaking his head, Carlos agreed, "We must get that book. In the wrong hands..." Carlos was unable to finish.

"Not the wrong hands, anyone's hands here on this side would be the wrong hands. Come-on let's go, we need to watch him." I said. "Last-time it was in his coat, he has to take the coat off sometime."

It was twilight outside, that beautiful time when the world appears to slow down, like a switch has been flipped. People running about, slowed their steps, looked around them, enjoying the last rays of the sun in the blue sky.

Mr. Ferguson, stretched. Slipping his jacket off, he placed it on the chair. Looking outside, he checked his watch, then started for the door.

I slipped into the room. Carlos was standing by the exit Mr. Ferguson walked out of. Even though the library was empty, I caught myself tip-toeing to the coat. Carefully, I started checking the coat's pockets.

It wasn't there. Where could it be? I couldn't believe he would hide it. I started sweating. I had Carlos counting on me, Margo counting on me. How could I be this stupid, so confident. I should have known my plan wouldn't work. The shaking started, to go along with the sweating.

Then I remembered his face, the look of fear. He wouldn't let it out of his sight. Not his sight, but maybe the sight of others. I looked inside his coat. There was a new pocket added. He had used staples and some cloth to create the new, inside pocket. I reached in and quickly withdrew my hand, fingers on fire.

I caught myself blowing on them, then nervously laughed. My fingers weren't really on fire. Looking around, I found a glove left by one of the rugrats. Squeezing my hand into it, I reached in and grabbed the book.

Pulling it out, I almost dropped it. The book was slippery, almost like a fish trying to slip out of my grasp. Holding the book, I turned to signal Carlos it was time for step two, except Carlos wasn't there.

Stepping outside the kids' room, I saw Mr. Ferguson as he closed the doors. The doors Carlos was supposed to be standing in front of, instead of outside. He was gesturing, and I could hear him explaining that he had left his backpack inside. Mr. Ferguson said, "Come back tomorrow." Then locked the doors.

Carlos started knocking, then banging on the doors, still asking to get his backpack. Mr. Ferguson turned ignoring him and turned off the lights.

I noticed Carlos didn't have his backpack. He really did leave it. With Mr. Ferguson's attention focused on the door and keeping an agitated Carlos out, I quickly moved out of the reading room to the fiction section, Large Print the sign stated. There, on the floor was Carlos' backpack. As I opened it, the book, the only way I can describe it is it jumped, it leaped from my hand to smack down on the floor. BOOM! The sound the book made when it landed was so loud I swear the entire library shook.

"Who's there?" Mr. Ferguson said, walking away from the locked exit.

Breathing heavily, hands shaking now, I was in trouble and couldn't get out. How stupid this idea, why did I even think I could do this. Come in, save the day, I wasn't that guy. I was a nobody, nothing special just a kid.

Suddenly, a scream, a guttural animalistic wail broke the silence. The scream again, closer this time woke me out of my fear induced stupor. Bending down, grabbing the book with my gloved hand, I slipped it into the backpack, and walked backwards, slipping behind a steel bookcase.

"Where is it, where have you gone." Mr. Ferguson whispered as he moved about the reading room. "You were here, in my pocket, why did I take my coat off. Stupid, Stupid, Stupid," each word followed by a loud smack, as if Mr. Ferguson was hitting himself. "Why, why does this always happen to me. Something wonderful, beautiful comes into my life and then I ruin it. My writing, my job, even my relationship with Kitty, I ruin them all!"

Closer now, I heard the shuffle of Mr. Ferguson's feet. Taking another step backwards, I felt the backpack being pulled and would have fallen if I didn't grab the bookshelf to steady myself. The backpack again jumped, trying to drag me down to the ground.

The next aisle over, I heard, "Yes, I feel you. Like when you called to me from the reading room, under the gift chest. You're near."

A book dropped from above, cracking me in the head. More books fell, forcing me to drop on the ground and crawl away, dragging the backpack with one hand. Glancing back, books were dropping and flying from the top shelf of the metal bookcase. Then there was a hand, followed by another. Finally, the bald head of Mr. Ferguson appeared. He was squeezing through the bookshelf. His face was contorted, in the low light of the library, it looked like worms were crawling underneath his skin, squirming and wriggling. It was cool and sick at the same time.

sign saying Emergency Exit. Running full speed, I slam into the bathroom door. Grabbing the knob, I twist to the right, then left but it wouldn't open. It was locked. Collapsing in front of the door, how could it be locked, it wasn't last time. Someone locked, it, Did Mr. Ferguson know? Is that how he planned to capture me?

I looked up as Mr. Ferguson came around the corner. He slowed now, straightened his crooked tie and smiled. His fingers flexed, his heavy breathing came under control. "Now" he said, the smile even bigger on his face. "There is something of mine that you have. I want it. Give it to me now!" He yelled as he started moving toward me.

"No", I whispered. Then louder, I said, "NO! This is not yours, I don't know how you made it to the Library, the other one, but this book belongs there, not here. It's too powerful"

Ferguson stopped, "The other what? What are you talking about. Yes, that book is special, but I found it under the gift treasure chest, there." he pointed back over his shoulder, toward the reading room.

I stood up and said, "True or not this doesn't belong here and I'm going to..."

"What?" Mr. Ferguson whispered, "What you are going to do is give me that book right now." extending his hand, palm up waiting for the book.

There was nowhere for me to go. Resigned, I threw him the backpack. Mr. Ferguson smiled, bending down opening it. Notebooks and other items came out, flying everywhere as he dug further in. What looked like a smushed sandwich came next, followed by soccer socks, smelly he quickly threw them away, wiping his hands on his jacket. He then tipped it over, I took a deep breath, them charged Mr. Ferguson.

Well that was my plan, but I only took one step when, two hands grabbed my shoulders, and pulled me back. I admit, I screamed. The scream slowly died after I landed on my butt, sliding across the bathroom floor, bouncing into a stall door with a thud.

I looked up and saw Carlos pushing the door closed, Margo ready to turn the lock. I saw Mr. Ferguson, realizing I had tricked him, he started hitting himself about the head, thwack, thwack. I could hear him saying, "Stupid, Stupid". The door closed.

Margo, locked the door with a click. I stood up, my legs shaking from the excitement. I made it partway when Carlos grabbed one arm, Margo the other and hauled me up off the floor. Both hugged me, and I smiled, relief on our faces.

Stepping back, Carlos was patting me on the back, "Great Job Thomas. Wow, yes very brave!"

"Yes, but the book we lost it." Margo said sadly.

"Actually, no we didn't" I said. Walking over to sink, I grabbed a few towels, not sure if they would help, then started to reach behind me, but Carlos AND Margo were watching. I said, "Excuse me," then went into the stall. I loosened the belt on my pants, then came back out. In my hand wrapped in paper towels was the book. I could not make out the muffled words, but the book was still talking, trying to convince me of something.

Margo clapped, smiling and said, "But how where was it?"

Smiling a bit, I said, "Well I hid it where I was hoping he wouldn't find it, down the back of my pants."

Both laughed at this, but we were interrupted by a scratching, then pounding on the door. Finally sobbing, and pleading as Mr. Ferguson begged, "Please come back, please help me. I need you, I had it all, please don't leave me!"

Carlos looked confused at Margo then me, "Who is he talking to?"

"The book," I whispered feeling sad. I didn't say anything, but I felt sad for Mr. Ferguson. He was trying to talk to the book, but it was ignoring, no rejecting him. I knew for some reason that it was rejecting him, it didn't move or buck in my hand, just acted like a normal book.

Carlos waved his hand in front of my face, he had been talking. "Well the plan was a success," he said.

I shook my head saying, "Yeah, well it almost didn't work." Turning to Margo I continued, "Thank you for coming back. But how did you both get in here?"

Margo smirked, crossing her arms, then pointing a finger at Carlos, she said, "I heard him crying your name repeatedly, Thomas, Thomas. I knew that couldn't be good."

Carlos, shock on his face, raised his hand shaking it back and forth in front of Margo, "No, no, no, that is not what happened," turning to me, Carlos continued. "First, I was yelling, not crying, to warn you Thomas. That's when Margo came running, asking what happened, if you were hurt, she was really concerned for you my friend," he said, patting me again, and winking at Margo.

Margo, shrugged, turning to me. "Well, you hurt?" she asked, punching me in the arm.

"I am now." I said rubbing where Margo punched me. "But how, how did you make it in?"

It was Margo's turn to look sheepish. "Well, there is this thing called the Internet, you may have heard of it. And a place called YouTube, you can learn anything on there. From applying spackle, playing guitar, or picking a lock."

"You picked the lock!" I was surprised and impressed. Carlos, stepped forward, putting his arm around Margo, then looking at me, "Our Margo has many hidden talents, many."

He continued to look at me, and I knew there was more in those words than what was said. He was allowing, no asking me to be a part of their club, to be friends not only with him but Margo, who he protected like a little sister I realized. Smiling, I said, "Yes, yes she is."

"Group hug!" Carlos said suddenly, grabbing Margo and I, crushing us in his arms.

A loud thud followed quickly by a second drew our attention back to the bathroom door. The door was still closed, but looked off, crooked. They heard whistling, a familiar tune, Whistle while you work, and then another thud, and we saw something poke through the door. It looked like a spike. I asked, "What is..."

Margo said loudly, "Axe, he found a fireman's axe!"

Thud, this time I could tell Margo, was right, half the axe was sticking through the door. I could hear Mr. Ferguson grunting on the other side as he was trying to extract it for another swing.

The axe made a pop sound as it was removed. We all screamed as the axe was replaced by Mr. Ferguson's sweaty smiling face. "Got you!" He said, laughing maniacally.

Then disappeared as the axe came back through, whack!

We looked around, but there was nothing, no window or even a closet to hide in. Nowhere for us to go. I staggered, holding my head, feeling nauseous. I looked up and saw Mr. Ferguson's hand, now through the hole the axe made, scratching at the door lock, attempting to open it. I grabbed Carlos and Margo, who also looked sick, and pushed them into the stall, locking the door behind me. It wasn't much but that was all the protection we could find.

Suddenly, the lights shined brightly, then dimmed. Everything became blurry, like when looking at dirty fish tank. I felt a sharp pain in my head, I could tell Margo and Carlos were feeling the same. It was like Mr. Ferguson had taken the point of the axe and was slowly boring a hole into our heads.

I started to see things, flashes of colors, shapes and then the stall walls and door became translucent. There were waves rolling across it and I could see through. It looked like water. Then I saw the things, things swimming in the water. Suddenly one of the things noticed us, and started swimming faster and faster, getting closer and closer.

I couldn't tell what it was, but I could see the teeth, row upon row of teeth like a shark. But then this shark, not-a-shark, reached out with arms and hands instead of fins. I squeezed Carlos and Margo.

Then like a switch was flipped, the lights went out, a pop and the lights returned, and with it my nausea and headache disappeared.

Still holding hands, we looked about, the stalls no longer around us, just an outline where they should be. The bathroom door was open, standing in the doorway was something I could identify. Standing at about two feet tall, with black boots, brown pants and a blue tunic, I knew him well. He was found in most Upstate gardens, and around the world. The red hat on top, was exactly like all the others I had seen. The gnome was stretching on his tippy toes, as he placed an Out-of-Order sign on the bathroom door.

"We made it!" Carlos said, relief in his voice.

"AH!" the startled gnome said, dropping the sign. Turning he raised a finger wagging at the three, "Not nice. Not nice at all to scare me like that."

His voice was bigger than his body. Instead of the squeak I expected, it was deep and low. I admit I was a bit jealous of it. If I had that I wouldn't need any additional RRRRs when talking to Margo.

Clearing my throat, I said "Sorry, we didn't mean too. Actually, I wasn't sure this would even..."

But didn't get a chance to finish because from behind I heard someone else clearing their throat. It was our turn to jump and say "AH!", we turned, each in the other's way, all arms and legs, but somehow, we kept each other from falling. Behind us was the Librarian. scowling at us.

Surprised, but not scared, I looked at the walls behind the Librarian. They were covered in symbols of red paint. Complicated and seeming haphazard, but as I studied them my mind swirled, starting to make connections. I understood why the squiggly line was followed by the round fat toad-like blob, even though I didn't know what that meant.

I then looked at the Librarian, a paint brush in one hand, deep red paint staining the bristles, in the other she held what looked like a skull. Which of course it could not be, my brain was just saying telling me that. But that wasn't the most disturbing thing, it was the eyes in the skull, turning to each of us. I could feel them scowling like the Librarian. I wondered if what I thought was red paint was paint after all.

"Guess the wards really are weakened here" the gnome tssked. "About time we strengthen them."

Carlos stammered, and started to say something but his voice croaked. Margo took up the attempt to explain, but she didn't do any better, sounding like a wounded bird, she squawked.

Deciding talking would not work, I held out my paper towel wrapped package. The Librarian didn't seem happy with that. Taking a deep breath, I unwrapped the Book, holding it out with my left hand.

This time not only my arm, but my whole body was on fire. The Book talked to me, explaining all the things I could do with it. The Book showed me how to take my revenge on Stanley and never be bullied again but do the bullying. Fear was the answer, I needed to have the other students fear me. Have those that I cared for be protected, he showed my mother, not working for once. Spending time with me.

"No," I quietly told the book.

The Book explained how he could help me find love. He showed me Margo first, then he showed me my Father. "No," I said louder.

The Book then turned to threats, it would be my downfall. It would take everything away from me, including my new friends. The hate that emanated from the book was powerful. The fire I felt became a furnace, I was burning, any minute I was going to burst into flames. The book was trying to destroy me.

Then I felt a hand on my shoulder, Margo, at my side, my other shoulder another hand, Carlos. I smiled.

Glass shattered, not in the bathroom but in my mind. I felt the book leave my hand, as the Librarian took it. I almost collapsed; it if wasn't for Margo and Carlos I would have. I was sweating, but the queasy feeling in my stomach left.

Wiping the sweat from my face, I said "Thank you." To Carlos and Margo. "If not for you, I think I may have lost it." Both silently squeezed my shoulders.

The tinkling of crystal brought all eyes back up to the Librarian. Shaking her head, the crystal eyeglass chain she wore swinging, I thought oh no, this was it. We're getting the boot again.

But it was the gnome behind us who said, "The Librarian doesn't think so. Perhaps there is more to you, the three of you. Interesting, this will take some studying on my part. A wolf, A Sidhe, A Norman, I wonder where to start, of course the..." The gnome certainly had more to say but was interrupted by Margo, turning she said, "Wait, what, what was that, a Sith? I mean I know it from Star Wars, but..."

The gnome, looking annoyed at being interrupted, crossed his arms laying them on his belly he laughed, "S-I-D-H-E, child, Sidhe, the Gaelic word for the fairies."

Margo, her mouth dropped looking at the gnome, then quickly stepped forward, and wrapped him in her arms, lifting him off the ground in a full body hug. "Well, ah excuse me but this is a bit unseemly.", he said as his face turned as red as his cap.

Carlos started laughing. "All this time, never did you think of asking someone for help. How simple, how wonderful, to finally know what you are Margo!"

"Yeah!" I chimed in. "A Sith." Margo dropped the gnome, who gracefully landed on his feet like a cat. This time I saw the punch coming, and smiled, hands up "Sidhe Sidhe, fairy princess. I was kidding."

"Yes," Margo said, a magnificent smile spreading across her face, "I'm a Sidhe and don't forget it. Now I know what I need to study..." But her smile quickly disappeared, remembering. "I'll never know anything because we have been banned. Never know what this means or where I should start. Even if there are more of my kind."

The tinkling of the Librarian's glasses brought all eyes to her. She looked down at the book, then at the group of us. Slowly, she reached a hand out toward Margo, who raised her hand, palm up, and her library card dropped into her hand. The librarian turned to Carlos giving his back as well.

"Oh, Faolan will be happy to talk to you," the gnome said. "He's in here every week, hmm no every month, well not sure, time is hard to keep track of. But anyway, he comes here a lot, I'm sure he'll help."

The smile returned to Margo's face, a matching one appeared on Carlos. Carlos turned and crushed me in a big hug. With my arms trapped, he then kissed me on each cheek. Carlos said, "Thank you, if not for you and your bravery, I wouldn't have this chance." Turning to the gnome, he placed his arm around him. "Let us talk my friend." he said, rolling his RRRs, making the word frrrrriend. Walking out into the Library he asked, "Have you ever heard of a werewolf that didn't eat meat?"

The gnome shook his head negatively, saying "No not, hmmmm wait in the 14th century there was a Were king. Not a wolf, a Were Rabbit, but yes I believe he..."

Carlos asked "Rarebit?"

The Gnome groaned, "Ah youth, all these gadgets you have has killed your brain, WERE-RABBIT." The conversation died away as they made their way into the Library.

For a second time I was surprised as Margo crushed me, hugging then quickly kissing me on the cheek, sadly only one cheek. I wouldn't have thought it possible, but that kiss surprised me more than Carlos. Margo then chased after Carlos and the Gnome, questions already bubbling from her lips.

The tinkling of glasses again broke my reverie. Turning, the Librarian looked at me, then nodding her head up and down, she extended her hand. I never shook a ghost's hand before but was ready for a first time. Slowly I brought mine up, but instead of shaking, she deposited my very own library card. I looked at it, turning it, the image on it was of the Library and not the Library. It would change, almost like it was showing you what it looked like throughout the years. Still staring at it I mumbled, "Thank you."

I looked up as the Librarian who turned, taking the book and wrapping it back in the paper towels then placing it in a bag on her hip. She dipped her paintbrush into the skull and went back to writing, more symbols on the wall.

As I walked out, I turned, clearing my throat to get the Librarian's attention. Then said, "I don't believe Mr. Ferguson, was the one who stole the book. He didn't know about the Library, he said he found the Book. Also, please be careful with it. That Book, well it spouts lies. I know it wants something, searching for release maybe. Just wanted you to know, not sure how the book made it to my library" I stopped, feeling the card in my hand. "Not my, the other library." Looking at my card I added, "This is my Library now, thank you." Smiling, I walked into the Library knowing what I would research first. I had to go find Margo.

The Librarian watched Thomas leave, red dripping from the brush in her hand onto the floor. It's been a long time since the library had a bookwyrm. She turned back to the red stained wall, a frown on her face hoping and knowing the new wards would not be enough.

P.A. Curran's first story involved his storytelling Grandfather, a grizzly bear, and a large knife, typed on a typewriter when he was 6 years old. His Mother was called into school to discuss this "disturbing" story. With a reaction like that, P.A. has been writing ever since.

After years of writing Science Fiction, Fantasy, and Horror tales, P. A. has begun to focus on crafting stories that would be enjoyed by those most important to him, his children, mother and wife. With this publication, P.A. feels his Grandfather smiling, knowing the storytelling tradition of the Currans continues.

The Old Woman in Apartment 4B

Betty Badgett

My name is Octavia. I'm 79 years old and I live in apartment 4B. Some people in this building would say I'm nosy, a busybody. I've been in this building for thirty years. Moved in with my husband John right after we ran off and got married.

I wouldn't say I was nosy, just concerned about the goings-on in this building. These eyes have seen a lot, I can tell you. Once saw a man get drunk and throw his wife out the front door of the building, with only her underwear and white slip on. I watched from my front window. Didn't know what to do, since I had heard them argue so many times. The next day they were walking down the street together hand in hand. Old people use to say in my young days, never meddle in married folks business because one day they fighting and the next day they loving.

John and I had many happy years living here, but the good Lord took him home three years ago and life ain't been the same since. I spend most days getting up fixing breakfast, turning on the tv just in time for The Price Is Right. Love that show! Then I get my Bible out and spend time with Jesus. Gotta find time for Jesus!! My granddaughter Libby come by to take me to my doctor's appointments and to get grocery every week. Sweet child, my Libby. John sure did love that girl from the time she was a baby. Now she's a grown woman with children of her own.

I love to sit in my chair by this window and stare down at the people walking by and coming in and out of the building. Saw Mrs. Jenkins come in yesterday with a man. She's single and trying to find her a husband, I guess. I think to myself she sure won't find one like that. A woman have to protect her reputation. Can't have different men running in and out.

Mr. West in apartment 3B is a nice young man. Whenever he see me coming in with a bag in my hand, he come a running. "Let me get that for you Miss Octavia," he say. Wife walked out on him four years ago. They say she ran off with the UPS man. I don't know what's wrong with young people today. They just can't seem to stay together.

John and I had our rough times, Lord knows we did. But we stayed together and raised our daughter. Times were when John would come home with his head hanging down and a sorry look on his face. Laid off again! He'd say, "Tavia, don't you worry none now I'll have another job before you can bat an eyelash." He was a hard-working man. Didn't want me to work. "Just stay home and take care the baby and I'll take care of you both," he'd say, and he did too.

I worried so much about him working long hours, not eating much. Never knew he was sick. Kept it to himself. Finally one day he come home looking so bad. His face looked so tired. Sparkle in his eyes was gone, like somebody moved out. I knew he was tired and beaten down by life and hard times. I tried to get him to go see Dr. Hemmers over on 64th Street. He was our family doctor, but John said "Stop your fussing Octavia, I'm fine, Just need a little rest is all, and one of your delicious fried chicken legs."

That night John went to sleep and tossed and turned most all night. Sound like I heard him moan like he was in pain. I woke him up and asked him if he was ok. He stared at me for a moment and said "Tavia call an ambulance." I knew it had to be bad. We went to St. Adams Hospital and waited in emergency for hours until the doctor came to check on him. He had to have emergency surgery that night. I called my daughter Gail and she and Libby drove over. The doctor told us John had prostate cancer.

After he said the word cancer, I didn't hear anything else. Gail and Libby looked at me with tears in their eyes and asked if I knew. "He never said a word, child, never said a word." The cancer in his prostate was too far gone for treatment. All we could do was make him comfortable until the Good Lord was ready for him. I prayed night and day for God to heal him. Most days he ate a little, slept and took his medicine. I sat by this window watching life go by and praying for my John.

Time went by quickly. Winter turned to spring and spring turned into summer. I still had my John. Then in mid-August, he went home to be with the Lord. That's been three years ago, today. Gail tried to get me to move in with her and her family in Maryland, but I say "Long as the Good Lord give me strength, I'm gonna stay right here."

Like I said, I've seen a lot from this window. I watched children grow up and leave home. Seen the funeral home come and pick up one or two of the neighbors who passed on. I even saw Ms. Evelyn's daughter on her wedding day walking out to get in a long white limousine parked in front of the building. Evelyn and her husband were separated, but that day, he came over dressed in his tux and escorted his daughter and Evelyn to the church. Nice looking man that Mr. Ramon. Evelyn was crazy to let that one get away!! Oh well, what do I know, I'm just an old woman!! But that don't mean I don't know a good looking man when I see one.

Well, I guess I'll get up from this chair and go make me some lunch. Almost time for As The World Turns. That's a funny name for a soap opera. Love my soaps. They were invented for old folks like me that don't get out much anymore. They should call it As The World Gets Crazier As It's Turning. Lord, Lord. Only the Good Lord knows where this world is headed.

Betty L. Badgett is a retired Registered Nurse living in Walton New York for eighteen years. She has recently moved to Chesterfield Virginia to be near her family.

In 2012, she published three short stories in an anthology published by the Walton Writers group. She has also published four essays on the Waltonwriters.blogspot.com and the VillageWomenSpeak.blogspot.com

She has always had a passion for writing and reading literature. She attended the Huntington Memorial Library writing group each Saturday.

Since relocating to Chesterfield Virginia, she is continuing to attend writing workshop with the

James River Writers of Richmond Virginia. She has branched out of her comfort zone and is now reading some of her poetry and essays at Open Mic nights in Richmond.

She is currently working on a collection of short stories, poems and essays, which she hopes to someday publish.

Mrs. Lanyard Gets a Tattoo

Bhala Jones

"I think this is so cool, Mrs. Lanyard, you getting a tattoo!"

Martin, the heavily tattooed and pierced young tattoo artist grinned happily at me as I climbed up to sit, legs dangling, on the side of his work table. I was new to this and was pleased to find that Martin, who I had known nearly all his life, would tattoo me instead of some stranger.

"What did you have in mind, Mrs. Lanyard?"

Suddenly, I felt shy. "I don't know really," I murmured. "Do you have samples?" I regretted this the moment I said it fearing that the samples might appear on the flesh of hairy, living bikers or nubile young women so heavily tattooed that they didn't need to wear any clothes. So I sort of blurted: "I mean a sample book or something."

"Sure." Obviously I wasn't the first to make the request as he handed me a notebook full of designs. Anchors. Stars. Full and crescent moons. The Grateful Dead.

"Maybe a little rose on your ankle?" he suggested.

"Not exactly what I had in mind." I turned a few more pages. Skulls with and without crossed bones. Flags. Curvy little frames for the text of your choice. Animals...

"How about a small heart on the side of your neck?"

"Not really."

"A little bird maybe?"

"This," I said more loudly than I had intended. I was halfway through the sample book with my finger resting on the perfect design. "This," I said more quietly.

"THAT?!" Martin looked horrified. "Are you sure?"

"Yes, Martin, I want that."

"The screaming eagle?"

"With the text, please."

"'Born to be wild?'" He seemed quite shaken by my choice. "Tats are hard to remove you know," he warned after a moment.

I waved this warning aside. Now that I had chosen the design I was in a hur-
ry to get it done. "Do I lie down or do we do this with me sitting here? I want it
on my chest."

"On your..." Martin spluttered. "On your....um.... chest? But you're...I mean,
you must be...I mean how old are you?"

"I'll be seventy on my next birthday."

"Wow! You don't look it."

"Well," I said using my most formidable school teacher voice, "I am it. And
that's the tat I want. So let's get started."

For a moment Martin looked as if he might cry. Then he took a deep breath,
remembered he was a professional and said, "OK. Of course, Mrs. Lanyard. You
can have any tattoo you want. But do you mind my asking why?"

I paused before answering. I did mind, actually, but people were going to be
asking about it once I had it done so I supposed I might as well start talking.

"My husband. I want him to see it." And then, in spite of myself, I burst out.
"The son of a bitch!'

"Mrs Lanyard!" I had shocked the poor thing. "You were my kindergarten
teacher!"

"A long time ago, Martin, a long time ago." I sighed and blinked back tears
choking on a stifled sob.

Martin was all sympathy. After handing me kleenex and getting me a glass
of water he said gently, "He's cheating on you?"

"With the eighteen year old receptionist at our chiropractor's office. We
have children older than she is." Actually, I thought, I probably have shoes that
are older than she is.

"And you're getting the tat because you want him to know you're
not...umm.. ..past it?"

"I want him to burn in hell. But I'll settle for the tattoo."

Martin thought for a moment and a slow mischievous grin lit his face.
"How about revenge?"

"I'm _not_ going to go out and have an affair, Martin," I said firmly.

"No, no, I wasn't suggesting that. But listen: I've been looking for a new car
so I've been reading the CAR NEWS section of the paper every day. And yesterday there was an ad offering to sell a 2017 BMW for a dollar."

"A dollar? That must've been a joke, Martin."

"That's what I thought, too. But I decided to call just in case it was on the level. And it was! The lady who answered said she was sorry but the car had already been sold. She had had over three hundred calls and she seemed happy to share the reason she had sold the car for a dollar. You see, it was her husband's car and she had discovered he was not out of town on business but out of town with his secretary." Martin grinned slowly. "So, Mrs. Lanyard, I was thinking...Doesn't that bright red Porsche I've been seeing around town belong to your husband?"

I thought for a moment about how Leonard loved that red car. And for another moment about the fact that Leonard was going out of town next week supposedly on business but probably with her. I thought about how silly it had always seemed to have part of the family assets in my name. Until now. All that thinking took me about ten seconds.

I smiled, somewhat wickedly I hoped.

"You're going to do it!" Martin crowed, now grinning broadly.

"Martin, you genius," I said holding up my hand for a high five, "if you've got a dollar, I've got a bright red car!"

Bhala Jones lives in Oneonta, NY and is a published poet. She has recently started on a series of short stories, some of which are funny. This is a mystery to herself and others.

The Two Rings
Yumiko S.

M y husband and I bought a set of simple wedding bands just before we finally decided to get married. Our choice was categorized as 'Comfort
Fit', lacking the sharp edges. I chose one which is slightly larger for more com-
fortability. Sometimes it gets loose when my fingers are cold. But I have come
up with a solution: I put on another ring on top of the band. It is the ring I gave
to my mother before leaving my motherland.

My husband wondered aloud yesterday again: "Why did you wear the wedding band for pheasant hunting?" I don't know. I was excited to be going out
in the nature with my husband, and I couldn't leave behind the symbol of our
mutual love.

It was earlier, before dawn, when we first arrived on the field. The ink-
blue sky shifted into the tinge of steel gray. The reddish orange light gradually
pushed the darkness away. We walked a lot in the fresh morning air.

But the debris of grass seeds! They stuck on my boots and pants legs. Before
heading back to our car, I slapped with my hands to let them loose. I saw the
flicker of the ring in the air. I had forgotten that I didn't have my mother's ring
on top that day. It disappeared, was lost among the tall brown grasses. I looked
for a while and then gave up with a quiet sadness.

I have the ring back, though. My husband and my father-in-law went to a
rental store the next day before going pheasant hunting together to the same
area. My patient husband ran the metal detector, and he heard a slight murmur.
With more effort he retrieved my wedding band. I cried the first time since I
lost my wedding band when I saw what he brought back.

The other ring? That was lost once, too. When my sister was coming to the
States to see my husband and me, somehow in a last minute frenzy, she lost it
when she was getting into a taxi. About three months later, I received an air-
mail from my sister. There was the once-lost ring wrapped in tissue paper and a
note explaining that while playing outside my nephew had found the ring in a
nearby ditch.

How Do You Like Your Coffee
Yumiko S.

I looked at the simple coffee mugs: so big. Basic and beautiful. I looked at them for a while, imagining various settings in my home in order to have a feel for if they fit into my life.

I try not to buy things, especially when I don't need them. However, I had a lucky discovery: there is a crack on one of the assigned mugs of my husband, all the way to the middle.

I suddenly got a mission to check that store to see what it offers. I quietly jumped up and down in my mind—I saw that they now had more variety. I like the black ones. It's simple. It just has a writing of "Coffee Therapy". Perfect. I bought two. It lets the coffee filter sit much stabler than my own red rose mug does.

I was holding my breath when I was presenting the coffee (mug, actually) and asked my husband, 'how do you like your coffee?' adding softly "mug" as he did not have to hear me yapping about the mugs.

Of course, the greedy materialistic side of me grew restless, and in two weeks I went back to the magic store. Of course, my magic store had kindly sold out the mugs.

Then I saw a box of chocolate I had wanted for the coming Valentine's Day. What luck! How do I like my coffee and chocolate?

California Fog, Winter of 1989: Story I did Not Tell My Mother

Yumiko S.

I told Mother that I stayed at Barbara's after her friend's party in San Francisco. I told her that it was rather a fancy, upscale party. But I did not tell Mother that I ended up staying under the same roof with a set of two men.

It started with a flat tire. Despite my insisting that there was something wrong, my escort kept driving and driving. Now we are out of nowhere clad in party clothes. As I did not know anything about fixing flat tires, I offered to take his picture while he was changing the tires. Ray managed to smile to the camera.

Now the thick Sacramento Valley fog was in. My friend Ray started to talk about his brand-new flannel nightshirt: Ray thought that he would not be able to drive me back to Barbara's because of the fog. Ray would let me use his flannel nightshirt, but I had to stay at his and Bob's home that night.

Finally the fog lifted. My escort changed his mind and drove me safely back to my friend's house. Feeling happy to be back and be by myself again, I opened the front door. Strange...I smelled coffee. I had made coffee very early that morning. But this cannot be from that coffee.

I wanted to calm down my nerves. I opened the bathroom door. Then I saw it: the lifted-up toilet seat. I thought I was imagining things until I heard, 'Hello Yumiko,' in a low voice. This could be from a scene in a horror story. But I did not run into horror.

It was Barbara's brother lying on the living room couch as he did not want to startle me. He calmly told me that his father was using Barbara's bedroom and, as they knew I was using the guest bedroom, he was sleeping on the living room couch. It was now three o'clock in the morning. I retreated to my assigned room.

At seven o'clock, I heard Barbara's Dad's hearty laughter. He was saying as Yumiko woke them up at two o'clock in the morning, they are waking her up and taking her out for breakfast.

Yumiko S. likes to read. She prefers to write than to speak as her communication means. She was born and raised in Japan. Her writing influence came from Japanese professors in her college in Japan, and her inspiration for writing came from the works of Emily Carr, a Canadian artist and writer. Yumiko's adopted hometown is Oneonta, NY.

I Miss You Daddy
Steve Clapperton

"I miss you, Daddy," Beth whispered to her image in the mirror-like pond. Her voice carried across the water, through the woods and down the valley, yet no one heard. A cold chill danced along her spine as she studied her face in the reflection. The makeup she had applied that morning was starting to fade in the hot afternoon sun. She ran an index finger under her left eye in a futile attempt to repair the damage. She wrinkled her nose as she rose to her feet.

Beth put her hands on her hips and stretched her back. Her hand slipped down to her waistband and fingered the knife her father had given her on her sixteenth birthday. Always carry it with you when you go out in the woods he told her. Beth listened to her father's words as the flock listens to the words of the preacher. His words were gospel.

A tiny pang of guilt struck her as she lit a cigarette. Filling her lungs with smoke she closed her eyes to savor the rush. Exhaling through her nose she opened her eyes and studied the cigarette. It reminded her of being a teenager. She'd sneak out of the house with a cigarette or two that she'd pilfered from her mother's purse then she'd meet the boys from over town and share a smoke behind the bus garage at the high school. It was the thrill of the forbidden that let her know she was alive. She longed to feel that again.

She always wondered if they knew. Her father had told her stories about his misspent youth. That is, before he left. Her mother just sat in the kitchen and looked at her. She never said much when her father was there and said even less after he'd gone. He just didn't come home the day after her sixteenth birthday. It was all smiles and presents and the next day, he never came home.

Beth often wondered if it would have been easier had he died. But he didn't die. He just left. Quit. She couldn't blame him, not really. She took another drag on the cigarette.

"I thought you quit?"

Beth turned her head, it was Donnie.

"Oh, it's you," she said.

His head turned from left to right before he looked to his rear.

"Who else would it be?" he asked, "Daddy coming to rescue you?"

"Daddy ain't rescuing nobody," she said before taking another drag on the cigarette.

"I thought you quit," he said.

"You thought wrong."

They walked in silence for a minute when Donnie stopped about ten yard ahead of her, just before the rise of a small hill. He turned and waited.

"I'm coming," Beth said as she returned the bottle to the small knapsack she had on her back.

"Did I say anything?" he asked. Beth started walking toward him.

"This was your idea," he said as he turned and began to walk up the hill.

Beth removed the baseball hat from her head and dabbed away a bit of the sweat that glistened on her forehead.

"This is supposed to be fun," she said. Beth quickened her pace and caught up with Donnie. His shoulder length dirty blonde hair was pulled back in a tight pony-tail and he was carrying a walking stick he'd picked up at the beginning of their hike. He poked at the dirt with the tip, sending up a small cloud of dust. As she approached, he turned his head. He wasn't smiling. It was a countenance Beth had started to see more often over the past few months. Her stomach muscles tightened. She reached over and grabbed the walking stick from Donnie's hand.

He said nothing as he watched her climb the hill using the stick to propel her. As the hill grew steeper, Donnie resorted to using his hands on his knees to push himself up the incline. At the top of the hill the couple came to a wooded area. He rustled his way through a small patch of blackberry bushes before coming finding a branch of an elm tree that would serve as a walking stick.

"Did you see this?" he asked as he pointed at the blackberry bushes.

"No," said Beth. She'd removed her hat again and found some shade under a maple tree. Donnie picked a large berry and popped it in his mouth.

"Blackberries," he said, "and they are pretty good, too." He picked three more and smiled.

Beth studied the bushes as she picked her way through the onslaught of barbs and thorns before plucking a handful off one of the vines.

"Are they safe to eat?" she asked.

"Of course," he said before swallowing three more. "My father used to make us go berry picking when we were kids," said Donnie. He started toward the path. Beth pulled a small sandwich bag from her knapsack and filled it with a large handful of the berries. She dropped the baggie in the knapsack and jogged to catch up with Donnie.

"That must have been fun," she said.

"Hated it." Donnie's eyes were focused straight ahead into the woods.

"Is there anything you do like?"

Donnie's chest expanded and she could hear his deep breathing.

He stopped his progress and turned his attention to Beth. A two day growth of beard combined with liberal dose of sweat and more than a bit of dust made Donnie look every bit of his thirty five years. He rubbed his face, leaving a small purple berry splotch on his jaw. Beth stifled a smile.

"There are a lot of things I like," he said.

"Really? I wouldn't know it from listening to you." Beth walked past him and started into the woods.

"I didn't come out here to argue with you," said Donnie. It took three steps before he caught up with her. "What did you mean by that?" he asked.

"Mean by what?"

"Is there anything I like. You know there are plenty of things I like."

"Really? Tell me about them."

Beth had moved into the lead on the trail and was walking backwards, facing Donnie. She studied his face. There were wrinkles developing around the corner of his blue eyes. Deep blue eyes, once they were inviting, like a cool swimming pool or a tropical ocean getaway. Now, they were more like ice; cold and unwavering. He rubbed his neck.

"I liked the berries," he said.

Beth laughed.

"What's so funny about that?"

She turned and quickened her pace before she looked back over her shoulder.

"I knew you couldn't answer me," she said.

Donnie trotted up to her and grabbed her by the forearm. His grip was strong. He'd grabbed her before, but never like this, never so tight. Her eyes narrowed and her jaw set tight. She yanked her arm away.

"Why are you being like this?" Donnie asked.

A fresh breeze blew through the treetops causing the leaves to rustle and a few to flutter to the ground. Beth looked up and saw a pair of starlings fly into a fir tree.

"I asked you a question?"

Beth stepped back.

"Yes, you did."

"Well?"

"I just wanted to go out and do something. Just the two of us, what's wrong with that?"

"Nothing is wrong with that." Donnie knelt down and pulled on a stalk of timothy and slipped it into his mouth before sitting on the edge of a stone wall. "Beth, why are we out here?"

She sat down on the wall.

"When we were kids we used to come out here, my dad and me. We'd bring a picnic lunch with us, just the three of us."

"Three?"

Beth let out a snort of frustration.

"See this is what I mean." She waved her hand at Donnie.

"You've lost me."

"I have a brother, but you wouldn't know that."

"You never told me."

"You never asked!" Beth's voice echoed off the hills. She cringed.

"And how many brothers and sisters do I have?"

Beth looked at the ground.

"See, two can play this game," said Donnie.

"Is that what you think this is? A game?"

Donnie shook his head.

"No, far from it," he said.

"Look, Donnie, this should be fun, this should be relaxing. Look around you." Beth's face was tight, she waved her hand in the direction of the path they'd just traveled.

"Maybe it's the company," said Donnie.

Beth let out a groan.

"That says a lot," she said and started back down the hill.

"Beth, wait, I'm sorry."

Donnie got up and grabbed her arm. Again. She stopped and stared direct-ly into his eyes. His heart stuttered when he saw the steel in her expression. He released her arm.

"Beth, I'm really sorry. Truly I am."

His face went soft, it was as if the thirty five year old man disappeared and was replaced with a ten year old boy. Beth looked into his soft, innocent eyes.

"Who are you?" she asked.

"I wish I knew."

"So do I."

The two stood silent in the path, an uncomfortable distance between them. Donnie's head was down and Beth turned away, failing to fight away the welling tears that rolled down her cheeks. She pushed them away and swallowed hard.

"I guess we should head back," she said and started walking back down the path.

"We don't have to," said Donnie.

"Look, it's obvious you don't want to be here. You don't want to be with me. So, maybe we should just end it now. Really. I'm good with it."

"So that's it? You just want to quit on us, just like that?"

Beth started walking down the hill.

"Beth, wait. Can't we talk?"

She stopped and turned.

"Now you want to talk? I've been trying to get you to talk for the last six months and nothing. Now, you want to talk?"

"Yes."

She shook her head and looked to the heavens. She was smiling and crying.

"You know, Donnie, I once heard someone say something about men and women. It was, oh, I don't know, something along the lines of 'men don't open up until it's too late' or something like that. I'm probably getting it wrong."

"What you are saying is that it's too late?"

"It's over. You know that, deep down inside you have to know that. You've been miserable for the past six months and it's been obvious to everyone."

"Who?"

Beth scowled.

"Who?" she asked.

"Yeah, who said I've been miserable."

"No one said you were miserable, it's just been quite obvious. You haven't made any attempt to hide it," Beth said as she quickened her pace.

"Please, stop. Can't we talk?"

"Sure, let's talk," said Beth. She stood still in the middle of the path, hands on her hips.

"I'm waiting. So talk."

Donnie laced his fingers and put his hands behind his head. Taking a deep breath he looked at the sky.

"You know I love you," he said for the first time. Beth's eyebrows raised at the words. She shook her head.

"All this time, the last, what's it been, year and a half? And now, finally, you say those words?"

Donnie kicked at the ground with the toe of his boot.

"I never heard you say it," he said.

"That's because you weren't listening."

"Oh, come on, Beth. I would have heard you say that. People don't miss those words."

"No, I didn't say it in so many words, but you know I loved you."

"Loved?"

Beth covered her eyes with her hands and took a deep breath.

"Why does this have to be so hard?" she whispered.

"What?" asked Donnie. "I didn't hear you."

"Nothing," she said.

"In order to talk, you have to speak so I can hear you. That's how it works, you say something and then I respond. In order for it to work, I have to hear you," said Donnie.

"Don't talk down to me," said Beth.

Donnie threw his hands in the air and shook his head.

"Maybe you are right, maybe this is pointless."

The sky grew dark as they walked along the path. A strong breeze picked up and a clap of thunder echoed down the valley.

"Maybe we ought to head back," said Donnie. Beth shook her head and they started to walk down the trail when the sky opened up and began to rain.

The two took cover under a small stand of trees and watched as the storm passed through.

The air grew colder and fog began to rise from the ground as they continued their trek down the hill. Beth walked three steps behind Donnie as they came to a small pine tree lined valley filled with a dense haze of fog.

"Did you see that?" Donnie stopped on the path and pointed into the woods.

"No," she said and continued walking.

He grabbed her arm. She yanked it away when she noticed a figure in the fog. A female figure dressed in a flowing white gown and slippers danced between the trees.

"Ssshh," hissed Donnie.

"Who is she?" asked Beth. Donnie shook his head.

The dancer stopped and looked in their direction. A smile crossed her face.

"Where are you going?" she asked. Her voice was low and quiet. Donnie looked at Beth and shook his head.

"We are going home," he said.

"Together?" Donnie shook his head. The woman walked toward the couple. Her figure was lean, that of a dancer, her hair was brown and pulled back tight against her head. Her eyes were brown and piercing. She stared at Beth.

"You know what you have to do, don't you?" she said.

A warm feeling of contentment came over Beth as she extracted the knife from her belt and slipped it between Donnie's ribs, twisting it just as her father had taught her. His eyes grew large and the surprise registered on his face as he felt his heart stop beating in his chest.

The dancer dissolved into the foggy mist and Beth wiped the blood from her knife on her shorts.

"I love you, Donnie," she whispered as he lay dying at her feet. Her voice carried through the fog and down the valley, yet no one heard.

Steve Clapperton has been writing for most of his life. Starting with a long lost play written in fourth grade, he continued to dabble in stream of consciousness essays well past his college years. After raising a family he began to focus on more structured writing including participating in various writing groups and the National Novel Writing Month. He lives in Sidney NY with no pets, though, if he were to have a companion, he would choose a dachshund and he would name it Pepperoni.

Faeries Wear Boots

Rebecca Welton

N ew York is nothing like home.
  Home is born from warm, steaming earth and piled in stone. It is woodcraft and witchcraft, wrought iron and rolling hills.

The nightclub across the street blazes purple and pink neon through the glass of the library. It's sharp enough to cut my irises and make the tears form, absent the warmth of candles, will o' wisps or the Cóiste bodhar's lantern. I rub my eyes and smear mascara about my tired face in a messy pattern matching that of storytellers and streetwalkers gallivanting not unlike the wild hunt from tavern to bar, go-go club to curb.

The door creaks and the cast of green falls upon the pencil sketch before me, illuminating coffee stains on Bristol paper and darkening the charcoal sky into a darkness only here could dream of. I know who it is without turning around.

Heavy footsteps that make the old floorboards scream beneath his bulk.

The scent of metal tickling my nose.

"Liam," I say quietly, my frustration evident in the tone I used, no matter how many heaping scoops of sugar I tried to muddle in. "Your glamour."

"They're drunk," he says, North Dublin accent rolling across the fields of my mind, pulled from the roots of the earth and the stormy sky, "They'll just think they're seeing shit."

"I can't make excuses for you when everyone else must follow rules," I twitter in response, Scottish and airy. Opposites that complement each other like rose hips and tea. He sighs and sinks into the armchair by the long disused fireplace. I know he's peering over my shoulder, lips drawn closed and pursed in sight and eyes lighting up the sketch I have nearly completed of the street below.

"Do I have to wear a glamour in the house, like you?" he asks softly as my pencil forms the entrance to the subway, appearing an antique arch rather than the fluorescent putrid hole it truly is.

"No, Liam." I sigh, forgetting the glamour in the first place that still rested upon my t-shirt clad bosom, reflecting green and purple about the ceiling. "Won't you take your coat off? It will wrinkle if you lay on it like that, and your robe isn't appropriate."

"Nothing's appropriate anymore." He protests weakly, sitting up. The sound of leather draping over upholstery, of boot heel on wood, of claws over bare chest mingle with the graphite on paper.

"Humans make the rules."

I hear his lips pull back from fangs with the popping and cracking of saliva over my shoulder and his sturdy chin is a dead weight upon my shoulder.

"We just have to follow them," he laments. The green glow turns toward the window, streaked with rain and draped in ancient vines. "And I just have to follow you, Mab."

"I simply can't be mad at you," I chuckle.

Even his voice is a light in the corner of my heart. It's birthed of lonely cobbled streets only imagined in fantasies by the drones of this "dream city".

Fairy tales. Legends, they call us.

I feel more like that's the truth as the sound of a wailing siren, more sorrowful than my banshees, pierces my ears and pulls me back from sentimentalism.

"Is the coach glamoured?" I ask abruptly just as soon as his hands found my hairspray shellacked locks.

"And correctly parked," he replies, "You worry too much."

"You're reckless." I laugh when a finger curls around the chain of the glamour. Sterling silver. I needed to go alone to buy it, given how the sight, the smell, sound, especially the touch of gold makes Liam recoil in horror, freckled skin rippling into mottled green and blue. Not only does it disrupt his glamour, but it would leave hideous red burns that faded to soft scars. His back is an angry reminder of just how humans treat their faerie tales.

They try to push us from their minds and memories, purge us with the cosmopolitans and speedballs.

When we emerge, they attack. When we follow our calling, they attempt to kill us and bring our bodies draped over their shoulders as some grim proof of a world not their own.

"You're quiet," Liam murmurs.

I turn and see him hanging his coat on the hook without needing to be asked, taking in the sight of the hills and valleys of suffering spread on his back like a topographical map.

Liam; my beloved. He's what some would call the most disturbing of my court. He's large, with the build of a strongman with a blanket of dark hair covering a broad chest and torso. He's clad in old leather, scented with petrichor and incense, from waist to boot heel. His strapping physique aside, Liam is unique amongst the Unseelie fae. Mortals who see him as he truly is are often driven into states of madness with these words upon their quivering lips:

Cóiste bodhar...the Death Coach. Driven by the Dullahan...

The lights flicker.

I recall the swinging of lanterns and screaming of men.

The torrent of red rain falling upon their twisted faces.

Their incredulous shrieks of "Blood, Blood!"

Liam's laugh carried by the wind. Lighthearted. Warm. A stark contrast to the evil cackle that those men had directed at me as I dared leave the tavern alone.

"Are you alright?" He inquires, turning around, even though he need not. His skin, the shade of soured milk and veined like stilton with splotches of green and blue nearly glows in the dim light. Dark red blood shimmers in dried rivulets about his neck like a morbid piece of ruby jewelry.

Contrary to the beliefs of the Seelie court and their chirping liars, I do not love Liam for his appearance, but in spite of it. There is something truly beautiful about a being cursed with a frightening appearance being so warm, and loving, and-

"Mab, dear?"

I blink in rapid succession, long lashes fluttering as I emerge from a daydream that takes us back to the rolling green hills, dew kissing the grass, and Liam kissing my shoulder.

"I think someone hit a pole outside," I reply when he approaches, "I hope we don't lose power."

"Well, there is always the newspaper."

As soon as the words of reassurance are breathed against my ear, his eyes are the only light in the room.

The glare fades and flickers like the death throes of a firefly.

Protests and intoxicated screams filters in and pollutes the solitude with unpleasantness.

Liam floats into my vision, lamplike eyes shining and wide and black mane long and wild and draping over my knees. I take a moment to appreciate the details; the full, dark olive lips, high cheekbones, elegant nose, even the small cleft in his strong chin.

"I shouldn't have said anything," I laugh. He joins in.

"Ah well, with how tonight's revelry has been, I'm not surprised." He says, still optimistic and bright as the phosphorescence of his gaze, "Should I fetch the paper and look around?"

"I'd rather you stay here." I murmur, directing my gaze out the rain splattered glass as cheers and roars echoed from drunken bar goers. Lips draw closed over fangs and press to my cheek, the flush of my illusory skin matching the smear of blood that feels sticky and wet.

"As my queen commands," he whispers. His boot heels clack as he crosses the space between us and hooks a claw in the clasp of my glamour.

I feel it lifted from my skin as I assume the mantle of darkness, of the Unseelie, of things that bump in the night.

Queen.

That's what I am, or what I am supposed to be anyway.

Ages ago I lived in the sunlight and dew, surrounded by blades of grass and thorns and draped in the petals of wildflowers. I was surrounded with delight, squealing, saccharine, zealous joy, and yet I was unhappy.

I think of Oberon, of the lies wrapped in platitudes and grandeur enrobing a bitter center like a year-old cherry cordial left in the sun.

He's in Florida, last I heard. He sent a postcard last week calling me his one true love in one stroke of golden pen and yet enclosing a picture of himself, tanned flesh and Speedo surrounded by mortals.

He thought he was harming me, but in truth he only made me happier to have taken that chance.

There is beauty in the darkness that withers in the false glory of the Sun, warm and dark, Blood and bones, soil and wet roses after a thunderstorm.

Liam galloped across the night in euphoric bliss, the black manes of he and the horses dancing in the night wind. He found me upon the crossroads that night, sobbing lavender upon dying clovers.

He offered me his hand, bigger than Oberon's, calloused from handling a whip, streaked blue and green with shades of deathly marble and talons that broke my ivory skin and issued in waves of apologies.

The coach was velvet, the outside ebony, but my will was iron.

"You're daydreaming," he says with a soft chuckle as I reflexively spring from my chair.

"I was reminiscing of the day we met," I admit, casting my glance aside to hide the glow of my cheeks. I hear him drop the paper and sweep me off my feet with ease.

"I swept you off your feet and then threw an entire cauldron of blood into the hollow, how could I ever forget?" he laughs, lighthearted as the lights flicker in rhythm to an impromptu tango across the nonfiction section.

He spins me around with a grace the pixies of the Seelie court could only aspire to and Oberon could never achieve.

Each dip and twirl, step and drag of leather boots, flutter of hair and rumpled wings is so much louder in the silence. His eyes bathe the room in a chartreuse glow, hovering in midair in circles about us.

Duran Duran interrupts the imagined music and I catch his jaw in my palm as his head drops from the air in surprise.

Cheers and reverie once again seems to spill through every crack in the stone, every gap in the window frame, jolting two ancient souls back into a world they are strangers to. There is a rhythmic knock from downstairs, the kind that doesn't come from stilettos on pavement or ding-dong ditchers. It only forms words to our kin, but to mortals seems overly complex and harsh on the knuckles.

I seek audience with the Queen,
Where heart and darkness deep convene.
Should knowledge of our kindred creep,
My very soul may Dullahan reap.

Liam quickly snatches his glamour from a shelf littered with disorganized copies of Dumas and du Maurier and extends a large hand to my smaller one, curling beneath his square jaw. I squeeze my eyes tight and clasp my hand around his arm as flesh, bone and sinew weave together with a sound most foul and unpleasant. He winces once, then is still. He brings a hand to my hair, weaving through lilac strands in a reassuring gesture.

"Liam, I could have answered the door." I whimper, peering up into a freckled visage recognizable as my beloved, had he been whole and human, a faint red scar where flesh was never meant to be joined in any other circumstance. A chain, silver like mine hung below, and from it a crystal red as fresh blood that reflected on newly flushed skin.

"Mab, I've felt far worse, and besides, you've worn that all day." He replies, lighthearted as ever. He bends down and nuzzles my forehead, nose tickling my feelers, and descends the stairs.

Glamours are a necessary and painful evil for some of my beloved court.

The banshees pass as elderly impoverished, wash baskets of garments hidden in carts and rags tucked in oversized handbags. The brownies as children wearing large hats or in some cases as small elderly men espousing wisdom on late night subway rides.

Liam has more difficulty. His transformation into a form deemed acceptable was always heart wrenching to watch. Some wounds are eternal. Some wounds were never meant to be closed, no matter how briefly. When our love was new, but a rosebud on dead thorns, I asked him, curious as ever, if he had always been as he is, if he was in any pain. He smiled sincerely, not the stretched smirk of an idiot permanently plastered upon his visage, as if touched by my concern and answered succinctly; yes and no. He asked me if that was alright with me, if I preferred he don a glamour when in my company.

He was so used to the bile sensation of discomfort he caused by his mere appearance that he asked the woman who had fallen into true, deep, passionate love with him if she was disturbed. I wanted to smack his head out of the air, to shout that I loved him for what he was. He was blood, bone, shadow, the mad cackle of a wild rogue in the night, the hoofbeats and wagon wheels; and I loved him. I decided to respond with a stern "no" of my own, which caught him off guard and made phosphorescent eyes widen larger than they already were.

Liam and I both found security, validation, and shelter with each other.

During the nights we rode about the countryside, he could trick witnesses and frighten aggressive ones into silence. We traveled in the darkest night before the dawn while the mortals slumbered, unaware, but New York never sleeps.

This is the cruelty of the destruction of all things "abnormal".

"Your hair isn't supposed to look like that." I hear him laugh from the foyer.

"Come on, man, the Queen said it was trendy. Punk isn't dead yet, Liam." A tired voice laden with a mishmash of narcotics replies.

I descend the stairs once I hear the heavy wooden door shut and lock. Fetching the kettle and placing it on the stove, I place a heap of white tea leaves and chamomile petals into a small metal ball with mesh to allow for steeping.

As I retrieve the tiny stool to reach a mug from the cupboard, there is the clanking of metal and a wet ripping and snapping sound, followed by a sigh of comfort.

"Well I'm sober now." The guest exclaims, his voice cracking into a squawk.

Liam laughs, then emerges into the kitchen, sweeping up both a clean porcelain mug and myself up. The mug is set on the counter and I am placed upon my feet.

"Are you feeling better already?" I ask, concerned given the painful process and the sensation that he describes as a blend of slow suffocation and uncomfortable itch.

"I am. Startling Finn brings joy to my heart." He replies, planting a peck upon my cheek as Finn steps into the doorway, gangly and wide eyed.

He's shorter than Liam, but taller than I; a description that fits the majority of beings, mortal and fae. His nose, ears, hands, and feet are large, and his face is thin. Round eyes with dark circles around them peer and me and a shock of violently electric blue hair stands up from his head like the crest of an irate cockatoo. He's clad in a denim jacket that appears to have been tossed in the dirt and covered with bright patches, a tank top, and jeans that make his stilt-like legs look bone thin. On his feet are sneakers that were lazily tied and colored with highlighters.

"Finn" I say simply, content that in spite of his bizarre hair color, he at least fits in with a specific crowd and isn't blatantly inhuman. I take note, in particular, of the small acne scars his glamour bestowed upon the dark skin of his forehead, and the slight paunch where his shirt was tight around his middle. "You need to speak with me? Please. You do not need to wear that indoors."

There is an exhale, and as soon as the faux gold chain leaves his skin, fur as bright as his hair begins emerging from his arms, legs, and neck. Soon, what appeared to be a large furry man with rabbit-like ears and piercing eyes stands before me and sinks into a bow.

Finn is a Pooka; one of four in my court. He came to this city long before us, finding it a refuge while Liam and I found a prison. Here he wasn't hunted for his blue pelt. Here he could be anyone. He could disappear in a crowd or stand out. This is the blessing of a shapeshifter.

"My Queen," He mumbles, shaking his head. "I think I saw a Seelie court fae about at Polyester's a couple days ago. Looked like a Sylph, but I couldn't tell."

Liam is beside himself with chuckling.

"Are you sure you didn't see someone in a costume? The Polyester doesn't seem like the sort of place a Sylph would visit," he says. A good point. Oberon's fae, when they "lowered themselves" to live among mere mortals would often frequent only the highest quality establishments. A dance hall with graffiti plastering the walls does not seem like the sort of place one would visit.

"Her eyes were like liquid diamonds," Finn says. "And no amount of make-up could make a face appear that flawless. I left as soon as I saw her."

"It may well bear some looking into," I speak up, punctuated by the wail of the kettle. Pouring hot water into the mug and adding the tea ball, the air is perfumed floral and earthy as the dried tea components are revived. "There is little that Oberon can do to either Liam or I, though. I am not slighted by his bragging in the least bit."

"You think Oberon sent her?" asks Finn, his bushy brow furrowing with concern.

"Of course," Liam answers, crossing his arms and leaning against the edge of the counter, "He still sends her postcards, you know? Thinks it will make her skitter on back to him. Tries to write about how much of a "beast" I am, while having the writing skills of a brownie with a crayon."

I chuckle.

A "beast". One of the many words Oberon used to describe my current partner.

"A grotesque testament to the decline of faeriekind."

"A reaper in the guise of a festering corpse."

Pathetic attempts to make me abandon my life, my Court and my love. Pathetic, lonely, and, as always, controlling.

If the Seelie King truly cherished his former Queen, if she meant to him as much as he claimed in the postcards, the letters, the mixtapes full of Police and

Crowded House, he would have shown this side when she was still upon the throne in the sun.

He would not have bellowed, not have boasted, not have struck or squeezed.

I breathe in and out as moments that I wish I could forget float to the surface in a sickening curdle. Liam's arms are nearly immediately upon my shoulders, calming me from the churning tempest and dragging me from a sea of memories best left buried.

"I'm sorry," I mutter, and a claw taps the pout of my merlot lips.

"So...say that the Sun King is spying on us, yeah, and this isn't a coincidence?" the Dullahan asks as I calm down with an impromptu shoulder massage, the bristly black hair of his chest tickling the back of my neck.

"He could find and shake down other Unseelie for information." Finn speaks up, "That's what I'm worried about. Kimberly has already mentioned changing the locks." The Pooka's informed, aware, and yet very human wife is generally a carefree woman, decorated with fuchsia eyeshadow and doorknocker earrings. If she was worried, perhaps this matter was more serious than I thought.

I make quick mental notes: Inform the banshees who will pass information from bugbear to barghest, spriggan to selkie; perhaps inform the mortal authorities of a stalker; ensure that the Cóiste bodhar is well maintained.

"I wouldn't worry too much about it." Liam says, ever carefree, "He may believe the lies the humans do of this Empire city and become swallowed in it before it becomes a concern."

His words are a balm that soothes bile and seem to even calm the apprehensive Finn. I keep the mental notes, but file them away in some cabinet in the dusty corner of my mind.

Liam is used to conversing with the troubled and worrisome. How anyone could say that the chauffeur of souls that pass beyond was some inhuman monster has always baffled me. He could easily snatch them up in his great arms, kicking and screaming, but he does not.

"You're right, love." I admit, once again having fallen into the worrywart trap, "It makes no sense to panic. Though, Finn, thank you for sharing this with us."

The Pooka nods, seeming more at ease and peers at the fragrant and freshly steeped cup of tea. I remove the mesh tea ball and slide the small decorative hive-shaped pot of wildflower honey across the counter. Nodding at the invitation, Finn stirs a heaping spoonful into the beverage and sips from the mug.

All fae of the Unseelie Court enjoy tea with honey, however, the variety depends on each individual. I prefer a brew of mature rose petals and Darjeeling with orange blossom honey, while Liam prefers pure lapsang souchong with the smallest hint of buckwheat honey and whiskey. Tea, be it herbal or otherwise, closes every meeting and leaves the visitor with a warm sense of peace, knowing that their concerns have been observed and they are welcome in the Court. I aim to make all under my care feel safe and cared for. Their duties are not easy ones and their paths even less so, and so the very least I can do as queen is ensure that they have a refuge with me.

Once Finn finishes his cup of tea, he departs with a bow and a promise that he will keep an eye on things and inform those among the Court that he interacts with of any possible infiltrators.

I peer outside, watching as he disappears into the crowd, becoming nameless, faceless, and unknown in this city of lies and dreams.

Liam shrugs and stretches his arms upward with a pop of overused joints.

"It seems like the power is fixed," he says, "You could finish that drawing that you started."

"I don't really feel like drawing right now," I reply, running a hand through my hair and sighing.

Oberon, difficult and wretched Oberon, was up to something.

How dare he attempt to ruin a happiness that I hunted with bare hands?

I glance up at the Dullahan, looking him over once again. The first day I laid eyes upon him he wore the garb he was known for; a long black robe, gauntlets and sabatons of black metal that appeared to glisten in the moonlight, and a wide smirk. A mutilated giant with a large, flexible, bleached spine clenched in right hand, and the leather reins of the horses of the Cóiste bodhar in the left.

He was a nightmare.

He was an escape.

He is where my love lies.

The bar crowd silences themselves for a moment before the roar of Tears for Fears splits the silence, jolting me from yet another moment of quiet meditation.

Liam knows that these moments are full of worry. They have chased us from the Emerald Isle across ocean and from Hollow to Haven and back. Rather than allowing me to stew in my own series of "what if's", I hear his heels clack as he moves from kitchen to living room and the tape deck.

One of the songs we've designated as "our song" plays, quiet guitar and breathed vocals. Liam's hand engulfs mine in a gentle grasp, pulling me close to a slow dance full of murmured phrases and reassurances.

"It's just you and me tonight now, my dear," he says softly, "How would you like to spend it?"

"With you. Always. It doesn't matter how."

It doesn't matter what the humans do.

It doesn't matter what Oberon does.

It's been that way since that fateful meeting when I stumbled into his arms and into this role. His hand slides up my back and claws tease the ends of my hair.

Soon our own music duels with that of the other "creatures of the night". For this moment it is as if we are in sync with mortals, rather than in opposition.

Dancing.

Smiling.

Kissing.

Falling.

When the leather sofa creaks beneath me I try to catch my breath, eyes dilated, heart pounding, cheeks lilac and waxy blackened wings crinkled like cellophane.

Rumpling fabric.

Trails left by lips upon shoulder and neck.

Tiny red scars left by nails.

Black curtains of hair shield our faces and, as the true night rises in the sky and the go-go bar quiets to wailed false names and scuffling of heels, true love overwhelms two souls and draws them into its rapture.

Skin bathed in green light.

Arms holding me tight.

I love the night.

These moments could last an eternity and I would have no quarrel or protest.

The ceiling dissolves into a blur of paint strokes and plaster.

Pale lashes flutter.

The music from the tape deck and from us crescendos and then fades.

The leather sticks to my sweat sheened skin and my hair brushes a smear of merlot from my lips to my cheek and the bottom of my t-shirt around my neck. I'm a mess, but I couldn't care less. There's a chuckle, a kiss, and a rumble of contentment.

Liam.

I love him. I love him.

I love...

I must have drifted off as the soft click of the cassette's conclusion makes my eyes snap open. I become aware of three things in succession: Liam is still resting, arms around my waist and head beside mine, his eyes closed and his breathing a steady pace; there is the faint sound of hissing outside the large window behind me; and a pair of rosy eyes are peering through the smaller one to my left. I bolt upright with a shocked, shallow squawk, startling Liam from his slumber in the process.

"What, what is it?" he asks, eyes wild and darting about as his head spins in circles and darts from corner to corner of the living room. He sits up and I hurriedly pull my oversized t-shirt down over my body, still staring at those eyes. I raise a long finger and point.

What are those?

Who is it?

What do they want?

Liam wastes no more time and I hear the rustling of leather and clinking of metal as he dresses and the subsequent slamming of the door as he, without glamour and black mane clenched in tight fist, bolts out into the darkness after the stranger.

There is a scream.

There is a crash.

Then silence.

I follow Liam, locking the door and holding the key between my index and middle finger. As I dart around the corner, my wide eyes widen even further at the sight before me.

The Death Coach, the Cóiste bodhar, glamoured as a beautiful shiny black Camaro with custom molding in the shape of a spinal column, and tire rims in the shape of crossed bones, has had all four of its tires slashed and was leaking air. Its driver, the Dullahan looms ominously over a whimpering figure, grin reflexively stretched wide and showing each and every one of his glistening fangs.

"Liam!" I call out, and he glances at me for a moment.

"Mab, please see to the horses." He replies through gritted teeth, "I will make sure this one does not move a single muscle."

While I am his Queen and could oppose what he says with ease, I know that I would have an easier time of healing the injured fae steeds. Deactivating the glamour is as simple as patting the chrome mane of the custom hood ornament as one would stroke a horse's mane. The illusion dissipates, and the four elegant steeds tethered to the large wagon appear, stressed and frothing with fresh cuts at their ankles. Upon seeing their Queen, the horses relax, bowing their narrow heads and allowing me to comfort them by stroking their muzzles and then tending to their wounds with fresh sprigs of yarrow pulled from the flowerboxes. Liam, meanwhile, continues bearing down on the shadowed pink eyed figure.

"I swear I didn't- "it begins, voice airy and slightly nasal, but unmistakably that of a terrified Pixie.

Once the yarrow began to take effect on the steeds, sealing their tiny wounds, I reapply the glamour by manner of spell. A wave of my hand, the murmuring of words in a language long forgotten, and the Camaro returns in a haze of black smoke. The tires appear to have never been slashed at all.

I turn my attention to the shivering Pixie and peer down at her. She's a fragile looking thing, small with eyes too far apart to be entirely human, a button nose, and a peach pout that quivers as if she is about to burst into tears. Liam isn't one to terrify without cause, but I cannot feel like this creature, usually the simple idealist of the Seelie Court performed this deed on her own.

"Queen Mab, please...I didn't do it. Don't let him take me in the coach!" she squeaks, and the tears start to flow, fat and wet and reddening her eyes further.

This is how I know she isn't a guilty party.

Guilty Seelie fae avert their eyes. They smile, secure in their deeds, too proud to stoop to sniveling and blubbering. This poor creature, this scapegoat, is genuinely terrified, and hardly looks strong enough to lift a butter knife.

"She didn't do it." Liam repeats, seeming confident in the truth of these words, but still keeping an eye on the Pixie lest she escape into the bustle of the city. I offer her my hand, which she eagerly takes, and pull her up to her feet.

"That she did not, but we have to ask some questions." I sigh, "Take it."

The tiny woman begins to panic, letting out a screech in anticipating of something horrid, before Liam very slowly extends his palm to her and raises a thick brow.

"Your clover, miss. Just one of them." He says in a much softer tone; the tone he uses with brownies, bugbears, and his own steeds. The Pixie visibly relaxes and pulls a tiny emerald green plant from the bundle tied around her neck, placing it in the center of my beloved's palm. She looks confused, but relieved. I can only imagine what lies Oberon has filled her head with.

"If the Dullahan catches you, he will take your soul."

Yes. That is the most likely lie that he spoon fed her with the malbec, mulberries, and tree sap.

A common misunderstanding, of course. Liam does not kill. Liam does not harm unless there is a dire need for him to do so. He does take souls, yes, but the souls of the dead, calling their names in the way I've heard humans speak to their loved ones hooked up to various machines in hospitals before the beeping of monitors stops.

He leads them by the hand into the wagon and brings them to their final destination, wherever that may be, joking and making merry from his perch at the front of the coach, his glowing eyes leading the way.

Of course, Oberon would twist "kindly shepherd" into "monstrous murder" if it suits this bizarre smear campaign that he runs against my beloved.

As for the clover, it is a mere token of gratitude that would ensure the Pixie protection from the darkness within the domain of the Unseelie. As long as we have one of her clovers, she is safe with us. As long as we have one, Oberon and his fae cannot retaliate against a woman that they believe to have been served a cruel fate. Liam closes his hand around the greenery and smiles.

"What happens now?" she squeaks, still vibrating with fear and hesitation.

"Well, first I gobble up your soul with these big teeth of mine." Liam replies with the single most blatantly joking tone he can muster.

"You're..."

"Of course not, little one. Please, come inside, tell us about what happened." I interject as I unlock the door and she shuffles in, her oversized pale pink Chuck Taylors scuffling along the floor. I close the door behind us and wonder what sort of tea a Pixie would like.

Something quite sweet. Fruity, with plenty of sugar.

"Liam, please fetch a sachet of that mortal tea...the Berry Blast sort, and the plain sugar. Set a kettle, love, if you would."

"Of course, dearest," he replies, his head floating over to kiss my cheek and his body departing for the kitchen. I turn my attention to the Pixie, who looks around nervously. "I do apologize for all of this, but I will need some information from you."

"But his majesty will find out...and he'll surely have me cast to the thorns," she squeaks, wiping her eyes on the sleeve of her sweatshirt.

"He will do no such thing. I promise you this," I say softly, and gesture to the armchair as I sit on the sofa. "What do you call yourself?"

"Camellia."

Liam enters the room with the tea in the tiniest "mug" we have; a large ceramic shot glass in the shape of a boot. He places it on the side table and sits down on the couch beside me. Camellia immediately stares at him in horror and her lip starts to tremble once more.

"Think of my Liam like a Cu Sith. His bark is far worse than his bite, and his jokes are even worse." I say, getting the Pixie to at least stop shaking for a moment.

"Hey! My jokes can knock someone dead," he replies.

Camellia gasps in horror.

I sigh.

This is going to be a long morning.

With each sip of the steamy sweet beverage, the Pixie opens up to us. She moved to the city from Florida in search of adventure and a new life. She works at a cute little old-fashioned ice cream shop on Mondays, Wednesdays and Fridays, and spends the rest of the time working at a department store makeup counter. She sold a tube of lipstick to a woman that she described as having "eyes like liquid diamonds" and, when the woman was signing the card receipt, she had left her phone number.

Liam's eyes widen with recognition based on Finn's previous encounter, but I allow the Pixie to continue speaking.

Camellia called the number.

Oberon, of all people, answered.

He threatened her, he lambasted her for daring to stray from him and welcomed her back into the fold with a proposition most foul.

Camellia would accompany the Sylph, whose name she did not even know to our home. The Sylph would slash the tires of the glamoured Cóiste bodhar with a gold-plated knife. Camellia would remain behind as a scapegoat, an offering, to the no doubt enraged and violent Dullahan. She would do this, or she would be cast to the thorns and the unnamable things that slinked about in its grasp.

Should she survive the "inevitable", however, she would be welcomed back home. A home that had treated her just as poorly as it had its former Queen.

She was a pawn.

The gears in my head spun as I try to come up with a reason, no matter how twisted, as to why Oberon would sacrifice one of his own, when I arrived at a conclusion. If Liam attacked Camellia. If he killed her, as the Seelie court believes he kills others, I would witness her butchering, become distraught, and return to his side. My stomach churns with disgust.

Liam catches on to the implications of Oberon's actions and his nose crinkles, his hand finding its way to my shoulder and rubbing gently.

"I'm so sorry all of this is happening to you," I eventually say, sighing, "You're welcome to stay with us as long as you need."

"But what about my jobs?" she asks, eyes wide.

"A friend of ours has a wife that works at the same mall, and I'm sure one of them could take you to the ice cream shop as well."

"Oh yeah, Finn and Kim," Liam speaks up, looking at Camellia and smiling "They're good people." The Pixie's eyes widen, and she nods.

"Kim Taggart? Does she work in lingerie and have really poofy blonde hair?"

"That'd be her," I chuckle. "You know each other?"

"She gave me a ride one night when I had to work late," Camellia continues, pausing and furrowing her brow slightly, "Is she...?"

"No. Kim is mortal, but Finn is a Pooka." The Pixie relaxes as soon as I identify the type of fae that our friend is. She still seems surprised by the kindness we are showing her; understandable, acceptable. I lead her upstairs the moment she begins to yawn and rub at her eyes, the true sign that she has calmed enough to relax. The guest room is on the second floor with a view of the skyline, a television, and a bed draped in the coziest blankets and sheets sewn by the skilled banshees within the court in a variety of colors and patterns. Camellia is ever so thankful and grateful. Despite her surprise, I see joy shining through.

She is what the Seelie fae are believed to be by mortals. Lighthearted and gleeful, innocent, sweet. She turns the channel to MTV and sits down to watch, pulling off her oversized hoodie and revealing a highlighter yellow tank top and green shorts beneath. Her lacy, peach colored wings flex and flutter, sparkling in the dim light. I leave her with a glass of water, a set of clothes from me to borrow, and a reminder that should she need anything, we will be downstairs.

Liam is tracing sigils in the air with a claw, leaving trails of red light floating in midair for a moment; a way of communicating a message to other members of the court.

"Finn's probably asleep," I say. "The shop switched him to morning shifts."

"He should get it when he wakes up in that case," Liam replies, concluding the message.

"Once our guest is comfortable, we need to know that Sylph's name and any aliases," I say with a sigh, reaching for the remote for the television and sitting on the couch with an unflattering but careless sounding smack from the back of my legs. Liam joins me and groans, rubbing his brow lightly.

"I should have expected something like this, with how you have talked about him and all the things he has done."

"Even I didn't know he would take it this far," I admit.

"Mab, whatever happens, I will protect you."

"I will protect you too, dear."

"I love you."

His head rests on my lap like a particularly bizarre cat as I lean against his shoulder, lazily running my fingers through his dark locks.

"I love you, too."

He pulls me against his chest, the hair tickling my cheek. In spite of all that has transpired, in spite of what may come, I feel safe and warm.

Liam's eyes close and eventually I drift off to the sound of the newly falling rain, the occasional car driving by, and an infomercial host describing the best thigh workout. Truly a New York experience.

I awake in bed with knitted blanket draped over me, feet bare and a vacant spot beside me. The aroma of sweet and tart bramble jam and something toasted teases me upright. Liam is awake and preparing breakfast. My bare feet touch the cool tile and my dark eyes open wide with the sensation. I slide on my warm slippers and shuffle out in the hall and down into the kitchen.

"Good morning, love," says Liam, clad in pajama trousers rather than his leather pants and boots. He spreads thick deep red jam over a warm crumpet and places it onto a plate "Would you like any coffee? Tea?"

"Coffee is fine. Is she awake?" I ask, sitting at the table and allowing my mind and body to slowly awake, wings still waxy and eyes still crusty.

"No. Doesn't appear to be. Finn did get the message, though. Kimberly will be over to take her to work." He licks jam off of his claws, takes a bite of his toast, washes his hands, and turns on the coffee machine.

Watching a Dullahan eat baffled me at first, but I am never one to question magic.

A thought comes to my mind like an illuminated lantern as the rich aroma of brewing coffee pirouettes through the air.

"Liam. We should go to the mall."

"Hm?" he asks, pouring both of us a cup of coffee and leaving the pot on the warmer should Camellia like any, "Oh...do you think something will happen?"

"I have a feeling," I say, just as I hear footsteps descending the stairs and the shining face of the Pixie in the stairwell. The oversized Black Sabbath t-shirt and leg warmers contrast almost comically with her pink shoes, but at least these clothes aren't dirty. I thanked being a similar size to our new ward.

"Good morning, Camellia. Would you like any coffee?"

"Would I?" she replies with a nod and Liam pours the beverage into a small mug, which the tiny woman promptly pours a significant amount of sugar and milk into. "Thank you." While her smile is bright, her hand shakes when she lifts the mug to her lips. She's nervous. Understandably so.

"Kim will come and take you to work, and we'll be right behind you," Liam says in an attempt to reassure her.

I am glad that he has agreed so readily to my plans, but not surprised. Liam must have that same feeling, that growing, wrenching sense of imminent dread that pooled in my stomach along with bites of crumpet and honeydew. Camellia spots the bowl of mixed fruit; the aforementioned honeydew, cantaloupe, pineapple, and watermelon cut into spheres, and takes a piece of watermelon for herself.

"Camellia." I say, "Do you think you can tell me anything about the Sylph?"

The woman abruptly shakes her head, winces once and bites into the melon.

A silencing curse. I should have expected as much.

A knock at the door makes all three of us jump. The scuffle for glamours begins as I put on my necklace, Camellia slides a chunky bracelet onto her wrist, and Liam disappears into the bedroom with the ruby pendant clutched in his fist. I open the door to Kimberly's concerned face.

"Oh my god," She exclaims, engulfing me in a massive hug and briefly lifting me off my feet. She's a tall, strong, emotional woman, and this is our common greeting. "I heard all about what happened. Is Cammy okay? Oh my god."

"She's not hurt, but there is a silencing curse on her, so Liam and I will follow," I reply, patting her on the back.

Camellia, or, apparently "Cammy", rises up from her chair and is greeted with the same bear hug. When glamoured, the Pixie was nigh indistinguishable from the average young woman of this city; her pink eyes now pale blue with matching blue eyeshadow and false eyelashes, her pale locks crimped and teased, and her lips decorated with purple-pink lipstick.

"I had no idea about all this with you. Oh my god," Kim repeats, her eyes wide and her jaw dropped. Liam emerges from the bedroom, shiny leather and black denim, and pulling his hair back with an elastic. "Yeah it's good that you two are coming with us. Nobody is going to mess with that man of yours, Mab."

I laugh a little as said man wanders back to his coffee.

"You should probably not go in pajamas, though, dear. Just a thought." He says. I thank the glamour for already applying eyeliner, mascara and lipstick, but stare down at my giant t-shirt, shorts, and bunny slippers ensemble.

No. This won't do.

I excuse myself to get dressed and mentally prepare myself for what may come this day. As I hike on fishnets, buckle boots, and pull on an off-the-shoulder shirt with my beloved leather skirt, I hear Kim describe how Finn was reluctant to go to the music store, given the situation, and how he would try to keep an eye on things until we arrived. A final adjustment to my winged eyeliner and a "you-got-this, Queen of the Unseelie" nod and I am out the door.

"Alright. We're ready."

"Ready to buy a new toaster and ruin Oberon's day," Liam adds with a firm, jokingly serious nod.

"New toaster?"

"This one still smokes."

With little other banter, we leave the house. Kim and Cammy enter Kim's blue Taurus and begin to drive to the mall. Liam and I follow in the glamoured Cóiste bodhar. The mall isn't far, and the parking lot is fairly empty given the fact that it is still rather early in the morning on a weekday. Once they park, the two women enter the department store directly. We, however, use the main mall entrance. Liam's glamoured but still vibrantly green eyes scan the few people present in the mall entryway, either lingering by the fountain, or wandering from shop to shop, unaware of the beings among them.

Bright eyed, messy haired children running with arms and legs flailing in the direction of the arcade, followed by their disinterested mothers, chattering about celebrity gossip.

A group of teenagers lingering near the music shop Finn works at. Among them, a couple in plaid occasionally holding hands and engaging in sloppy kisses to the exasperation of their friends.

A few loners, usually impeccably dressed and in fancy fur-trimmed coats.

Liam's eyes narrow a couple of times as glamoured banshees waltz by with their carts full of yarn and kitchenware, brownies skip up to jewelry counters with wily grins, and a Selkie perusing the clearance rack of a women's clothing store.

"Do you see anything?" I ask, peering up at him.

"Not yet." He replies, "We should go to the department store. That's where the toaster is, anyway."

I agree, and, amid occasional stares, we walk hand in hand to the shop.

Even when trying to fit in amongst mortals, we hardly fit in at all. Liam's staggering height draws eyes, our clothing draws more, and the fact that we are conducting ourselves as proper adults makes brows furrow. Some part of me wonders if we should have glamoured ourselves to be more the common standard, but I rather enjoy the makeup of the alternative scene, as well as how Liam's posterior looks in the trousers.

When we arrive at the store, we are about to head to the appliance section, but as soon as we are about to pass the makeup counter, we see Cammy with wide eyes talking with a woman most bizarre. She is slim and tall, with permed brown hair and frizzy bangs. She wears an earthy green blazer, matching skirt, black hose and high heels. The shirt beneath is also black, and a tan scarf is artfully tied about her neck. This all seems normal, until I catch a glimpse of her eyes, and the inside of her coat. Her eyes are almost multifaceted like diamonds, in a way no mortal's eyes appear, and standing out like a wounded thumb from the crisp pistachio lining of her blazer is a small pistol and the glimmer of something gold.

This is the Sylph we've been looking for.

This is the woman who Oberon has sent to spy on me and ruin Cammy's life.

Her fire-engine red painted lips curl into a condescending sneer as she mutters something unheard to the Pixie.

"Liam" I whisper to him, tugging on the sleeve of his jacket.

"I see her. We can't do anything until she does."

"We need to tell mall security." I hiss, trying to remain calm and quiet.

"I already have." Kimberly abruptly adds from behind me, moving a rack of lacy bras from the front of the store into the corner where lingerie is, "They're on their way, but we need to buy some time. If they weren't just bullshitting me."

As I am about to thank her, the sound of the cart jolts the woman's head directly toward us.

"Well, I...didn't expect this." She says, her voice a low alto, "I didn't expect to see this little snitch alive, either. You're very bad at your job, Dullahan."

"For the last time, I don't kill people." Liam sighs with exasperation. She laughs slightly, a haughty tone, then turns her gaze to me.

"You should come home, Mab. Enough of this...whatever it is." She says, waving one of her hands around as she approaches me, the stink of cigarettes making me crinkle my nose, "This...escape. This folly. You belong with us...not with...that."

As she approaches me, the memories come flooding back, unpleasant as ever.

Oberon opening his bed to a diamond-eyed Sylph.

The cruel, musical, breathy laugh she taunted me with.

Unpleasantness.

Revulsion.

I am not surprised that she has undertaken this task.

"I think I can say for myself where I belong, thank you, Delphinia." I reply, struggling to keep a neutral smile upon my oxblood lips.

"I thought you would say that. In fact, I knew it." She says, "I was told to coerce you into coming back home, but I see no reason why I can't force you."

Her hand slides into the coat and rubs along the edge of the gun's handle.

"Idiot Seelie." Liam grumbles, "Do you really think you can just go on a shooting spree in a mall until you get your way? I know that New York is violent, but I am pretty sure that is against any and all laws."

Her hand moves from the gun to the gold-plated knife.

"But those laws prohibit the killing of people, Dullahan. You, of course, are not people." She says, her fingers moving to flick the blade out with the sound of a spring.

Everything happens so fast.

Cammy fills the room with a rosy haze.

Liam's belt is unglamoured into the spine whip.

Skin and flesh are punctured.

"Stop, Police!"

Before I my mind catches up with what has happened, I realize I am cowering with Kimberly behind a rack of clothes with a gun aimed directly at my face.

"Ma'am, drop the gun." A man in a blue uniform says, his own gun pointed toward Delphinia.

The smart thing would have been to do so, to accompany them to the police station.

The Seelie court is not known for their intelligence.

She turns the gun toward an already downed Liam, and I realize that he is struggling in vain to remove the gold-plated knife from his abdomen.

"Ma'am!" shouts another man.

"He's not a person, you fool. Just watch. Just watch and see."

"No!" I wail, diving over to shield Liam with my own body.

It all flashes before me again; our meeting, the night on the emerald rolling hills, our journey. Everything we had wanted, everything we had built for ourselves. Freedom, love, and opportunity.

I remember our private vows whispered to each other as we drove by the Tarrytown Lighthouse.

I remember the first thing we ate when we arrived in New York; bagels, toasted, with cream cheese and lox.

I remember buying the house.

Moving in. Dancing. Laughing. Being truly happy despite being in this world far away from home.

The gun clicks.

The officers' guns click.

The sudden sound as a gun goes off startles me, and I expect to feel a pain in my torso, or blood against my body. I did not expect a splatter of it to land upon my face, and the sound of a body hitting the floor, nor the screams of shoppers, Kimberly, and Cammy.

My eyes open, and stare into Delphinia's glazed over smirk as red soaks into her green blazer. Before I know it, an officer is attempting to move me and ask me if I, or Liam am alright, and a white sheet lined with runes invisible to mortals is placed over her body. To my surprise, it is Liam that actually helps me up.

"Liam...I...you were..." I mumble incoherently once I nod to the officers through blackened tears. He hands over the knife to the police, who store it in an evidence bag.

"Wasn't real gold." He replies, an incredulous grin on his freckled face, "He didn't even give her a blade of actual gold."

"But the horses...they were injured!" I want to ask.

"How did you know?"

"Why would he do that?"

In the end, I do not ask anything. In the end, I pull him down by the shoulders and I kiss him until his mouth is smeared red and the officers' tired "Ma'am?" "Sir?" questions register in my brain.

We are taken aside and questioned by a female officer with red hair pulled into a tight bun and a hefty build, however, she spends more time writing things down than asking questions.

"Will he be alright?" asks one of them, "We can get him some medical attention."

I glance at the wound left by Delphinia's false-gold knife, which has faded to a small scar.

"Think he's fine, actually..." I say, nodding. The woman nods as well and returns to the other officers as they usher people from the mall and tend to the shivering Cammy.

"Actaea has done well for herself." Liam says casually as she puts her hand gently on the Pixie's shoulder, calming her and escorting her to a bench where Kimberly and Finn sit, equally shaken.

We are asked to leave the mall as it will close for the day. We do so gladly. Standing in the parking lot in shock, I begin to process what has happened as Liam's hands rest upon my shoulders.

"I can't believe this asshole ex of yours." Kim says, breaking the silence.

"I can." Liam replies, shaking his head.

"What should we do now?" asks Cammy, sounding lost and confused, fidgeting and picking at her nail polish.

"Ice cream?" suggests Finn.

It's a ridiculous idea. It's almost callous, but we all nod in agreement.

With the events of past couple of days; of memories wished forgotten of a past that I'd rather not dwell on, a frosty swirl of vanilla, encased in a hardened bright blue shell of sugary candy and topped with sprinkles seems like an excellent idea.

Cammy's boss is surprised to see her so early but given her horrified expression and the news report that is playing on the television set, he welcomes us in and does not charge us for the desserts.

While Finn and Kim stay behind with her and her boss, Liam and I depart for home. Although he isn't severely injured, and the wound has healed over, I know that being in glamour after such a stressful event is unhealthy for him.

Of course, it is only sensible to turn on the news report as I arrive, sinking onto the couch with a long, low sigh.

The police found a card in Delphinia's coat; a card with Oberon's faux name on it, his phone number, and information. They had coordinated with Florida police and the very strange sight of the human form of the Seelie King with his tanned wrists in cuffs and blonde locks hanging in his face plays over the announcement of his arrest.

Charges of conspiracy to commit murder.

Charges of stalking.

Charges of, of all things, embezzlement.

"How is that for fate?" asks Liam as he sits beside me, placing his glamour on the coffee table. Mine soon joins his and I lean against his shoulder.

My mind is still whirling. It is amazing how many things can happen so quickly, but I suppose that is New York life.

I close my eyes and sigh.

"I know that it isn't over, though. It's never over," I mumble. My lover's hand holds mine gently, reassuringly.

"Of course not, but I will protect you."

"And I will protect you."

A contented sigh leaves my lips and, for once, I do not reminisce.

I do not think of the green valleys, the woodwork and witchcraft, the roses with their gnarled thorns, the sodden and damp earth on the darkest of nights.

I do not dream of horseback rides, the clanking of iron gates, the streaks of red and the clattering of gold as we flee with the stars into realms barely understood by mortals.

New York is different.

New York is noise and neon, nylons and nonsense. It's not perfect, by all means, and its streets are littered by remnants of nights forgotten with people one can never forget.

The clubgoers will always be dancing. The shops will always be bustling. The world of mortals will flourish among us, devoid of imagination.

But on this corner, in this unwanted brick relic of an earlier time, in the warmth and darkness of den of the Unseelie court, there is love; true love.

A love born from two souls so utterly destined for one another that not this city, nor the wills of mortals, not even forces from the false and gibbering sunlight can draw them from one another.

As the news fades into the background and the sound of Liam's heart beating lulls me to rest, I know of one fact in this world of uncertainty.

I am home.

Rebecca Welton is originally from the tiny town of Roscoe, New York. She received her bachelor's degree from Hartwick College before moving on to attain a master's degree from SUNY Cortland. In addition to her full-time job as a Secretary, Rebecca also owns Doom and Bloom Designs; a small art and home décor business known locally for floral pop art paintings, colorful coffin boxes, and horror-themed pins.

Rebecca's writing is driven by the concept of "darkening the day and brightening the night" and she enjoys dissecting and twisting different genres, such as Romance, Horror and Mystery.

Rebecca is currently working on a novella loosely inspired by the life of Madame Marie Tussaud. She lives in Oneonta, New York in a converted textile shop with three houseplants, a hodgepodge of antiques, and far too many books. She is supported by her loving family and her boyfriend, Andrew.

Upon your marriage to a redcap

Tori Curtis

Listen to your mother, but think before you follow her advice. Interspecies marriages are hard to maintain, and never survive without compromise. No one can outrun a redcap, nothing can stop her once she's sighted prey. You're brilliant; she loves you. If she chooses to kill you, you won't be the exception.

This is such an awful thought, she won't be able to voice it. It is such an awful thought, you must never forget it.

Those first months will be the loneliest of your life, wandering the chambers of a beautiful stone castle out of your childhood dreams. You'll miss your family, who are five hours and an ocean away from you. You'll miss having real internet.

Stick to what you hold true. Your wife is strong and handsome, and when you consider what the men in your MBA program were like, it ought to be enough that she loves you.

She loves you so much.

Don't call her a dwarf, an elf, or a fairy. She doesn't think it's flattering, and she won't see the humor in being insulted. Call her a knave, a knight, and pretend you don't know the difference. She'll frown and there will be bewilderment in her voice, and you'll remind yourself (every day of your marriage) that she isn't used to normal people.

"I am a monster," she'll say, "And I have no sovereign."

"You have me," you will tell her, "and all I see is that shining plate armor," and a craggy face and shy eyes under a burnished helm.

When she gifts you a gelding taller than she is, better suited to a joust than an amble, kiss her, name the horse Bulldozer, then write your parents and your aunt Hatty a thank you letter for those riding lessons all those years ago.

You won't discover her hunting grounds until she's satisfied you won't get lost on your own land. The horse will notice before you do, pin his ears and dance so wildly that you'll wonder if there are panthers here after all. But nothing will jump out at you until you dismount, and then you'll notice the stench, so strong you have to tie him to a tree and investigate yourself.

Your sisters are a journalist and a historian; you know about impartiality and ethnocentrism, you know about culture shock. Wait until she's settled down at the dinner table before you start screaming at her, like your mother did, like your grandmother, like you always smugly insisted you wouldn't. Like setting a bear trap, say, "I found the corpses today."

Her eyes will go wide, she'll fill her mouth with buttermilk biscuits like it might save her. Say, "You told me the cable guy must've got lost."

She won't try to condescend to you or act like you're crazy. That's part of why you'll stay with her. She'll say, "You knew this was my life, love," and part of you will do the math, is always doing the math. Is this reasonable? What are you supposed to expect, really, in a marriage? Upon whose death do you part?

Say, "That's bullshit. I said I didn't mind that you kill people, not that you can just leave your leftovers on the lawn. It took nearly an hour to settle the horse." Sigh, look at the corner of the wall that's too high for one to re-mortar alone, think: either you fix this or you leave.

"Well, I guess it's stupid to keep getting meat from the store."

Use every part of her prey. It's the least you can do. Boil their bones to make a broth, and it will give your wife the strength to raise a castle.

Don't be afraid to cry in front of her. Don't let it get into your head that she is a monster. When you miss your home, lean your weight into her and take off her armor. Let her hold you until you are warm again.

Remember why you fell in love with her. Remember that she is strong and that she is loyal and that there is so much of her that is tender, even if it's under bristles worse than a stinging nettle. Tell yourself that she's only so harsh because it's kept her alive, and then kiss her chest because it can be fun, too.

Don't let her near your sisters unless she has killed first.

Don't tell your mom you take this precaution.

When you find out you're pregnant, everything will change. You've wanted it so long, but when it becomes real, when you have someone else to protect, it will feel different. The way people have spoken about you, pity more than judgment—*it's her funeral, girls make stupid choices sometimes*—you'll realize that's all over now, you can't take it back. People won't be scared for you anymore. They'll see you standing, pregnant, with your wife, resplendent and unrepentant, and they'll think you're consigning your baby to a childhood in a broken home.

They won't see your wife's giddiness, that she'll protect your family with her life and feed you with her hands. They'll see a baby naked on the floor, crying and streaked with blood as your wife changes his diaper. You can't do this alone.

Call your Dad. He keeps strange hours, and he's always had your back. Say (not too insistent, not too naïve, not at all unsure) that you love her, that you believe she's a good wife. Surprise yourself by laughing when your dad asks, all cop training, "Do you feel safe around this creature?"

Think: yes, like you had felt safe when the family dog snapped at Cousin Jimmy, like you could walk across the highway blindfolded and no one could touch you.

When people ask why you married her, laugh, gleam, say you don't understand why anyone wouldn't want to marry a woman with stamina and an ancient stronghold. Then smile, glitter, say it's not that at all.

Remember that you loved pulled pork growing up. Make your grandma's old barbecue sauce so that you don't gag thinking of what you're eating.

If you don't use what she kills, it will rot in the fields.

Pray every day on your knees. She won't understand this, but it will make you feel better. Remember the old martyrs. Remember that your devotion needs no justification.

Don't wonder if your children will be like her. When your son asks for a hat like his mother's, felt the wool yourself and kiss his cheeks. Your wife won't be able to go home for Christmas with you, can't leave her domain, so stand tall and take your children yourself. Call her every night and let them talk to their mama; juggle three passports and glare at anyone who looks sympathetic in the airport; teach them about baseball and hot dogs; when the pastor at your parents' church asks about your son's cap, say, "They wear them in his mother's culture. I made it." Don't ever let your children think there might be something wrong with them.

Invest yourself in your home, your family, your love for each other. Learn the best drapes to cut the cold, learn masonry enough to hold the walls together, learn to be terrifying as yourself and not as the redcap's wife. When she says how you've changed from your wedding day, be proud and not ashamed.

When your children run from the table and ask, "But are we eating *people*?," she will want to lie or apologize. Hold firm.

Remember your mother, put another helping of potatoes on everyone's plate, say, "There are plenty of children as would be grateful for some people to eat, so don't go complaining."

Hold their gaze until they sit down, and then spoon some gravy over their biscuits.

Learn not to make assumptions. Don't be surprised when she digs a hole six feet deep in the churchyard and plants a tree with a tire swing. When your daughter burns her fingers climbing the sconces, find the poultice your wife made and text your mom a picture of her wrapping your baby's hands in gauze. When your son says he wants to be a painter, slam your fist on the table and say there's no reason he can't do that and keep up the family business, too.

Spend an hour a day on your hair, be the most beautiful wife you can be. Love her. Throw dinner parties. Buy a hundred-dollar blow dryer.

When she asks why you married her, say, "You know that," and "I love you." And when that's not good enough, think about it, crack your neck, say, "You're the only one who's made me think, I'd rather see where my life goes with her than if I were just on my own."

If she ever raises a hand to you, take her cap while she sleeps and set the dryer on high.

Tori Curtis lives in beautiful, scenic upstate New York with her unsinkable wife (Bridget, Huntington Memorial Library Program Assistant) and their irrepressible dog. When she's not writing, she enjoys ignoring recipes and giving friends bad advice. You can find her @tcurtfish on twitter or at http://toricurtiswrites.com

This story first appeared in Iridium Zine, March 23 2018

The Meeting

Becca Wagner

Is this seat taken?

A question. The kind of run-of-the-mill question you could be asked countless times a day, especially if you were spending most of your time in public venues with open seating, the way he currently was living his life.

"Uh, no," he says, turning to face the direction of the voice. "It's all yours."

"You're American?" she asks, sitting down on the old wooden barstool.

"Yeah," he says.

With a laugh, she summons the bartender and asks for a bottle of Bulmer's. When he asks what kind, she says, "The red one."

"What's so funny?" the bartender asks, popping the top off her bottle and placing it in front of her with a glass.

"This is just so *perfect*," she says.

"What?" the bartender asks.

"It's the most quintessentially American thing," he tells the bartender, "to find another American at some random ass bar in the middle of London."

"Whatever you say, honey," the bartender says.

"I'm Kate," she says.

"Eliot," he answers.

She rambles on about getting lost on the tube earlier in the day trying to find her way to the Tower of London, her favorite attraction in all of Europe, which she has visited three times and plans of visiting *at least* five more times during this trip to England. She has a thing for Anne Boleyn, she tells him, not Henry. Although he is a fascinating guy with his six wives, she's more interested in the mysterious Anne that stole his heart and basically caused the whole English Reformation.

"So that's why you're in Soho," Eliot says and shakes his head, thinking that he should have known better, that any beautiful brunette with eyes that lit up like Disney World fireworks would only end up in Soho for one reason.

"What do you mean?" she asks.

"You like Anne Boleyn more than Henry the Eighth," he says. "You don't have a ring on. You're in Soho for God's sake."

She tilts her head. "I like Anne because she represents a powerful woman who wasn't afraid to go after what she wanted. I don't have a ring on because I'm not married and I don't like things that make my fingers feel claustrophobic. And I'm in Soho because I have one friend in all of England and he happens to have a boyfriend and likes to hang out here. It's the only pub I know how to find."

He ignores the fact that there are countless pubs in London and that she could have walked into any of them to order a Bulmer's.

"So you're straight?"

Kate laughs again, tilting her head back so long dark waves of hair cascade down around her shoulders. "I'm straight," she says.

For a moment, while Kate is laughing, Eliot wishes that he could capture the moment on the film reel of his memory to replay during the dark, lonely nights, but the smoke from someone else's cigarette blown in his direction makes his eyes water behind thick black glasses and he has to look away. When he can finally see again, the image of Kate's laughter is gone, replaced by an image of her sipping Bulmer's from the bottle and a bartender who can't seem to figure out what kind of girl has stumbled into his bar.

"So," Kate says, "what brings you to Soho?"

This is a question he had been prepared for the moment that Kate sat down.

"I'm a travel blogger," he explains, "and my current assignment happens to be about travelling as a gay man in the United Kingdom."

"And you were commenting on my obsession with Anne Boleyn?"

Eliot smiles. "I'm not gay. The guy who was supposed to write it ended up getting a new job, a real job, one that doesn't require spending all of your free time out of the States."

He tells her about his last assignment, doing the *National Treasure* tour of the East Coast of the United States, starting in Washington DC, traveling through Philadelphia, New York City, and ending in Boston.

"No shit?" Kate says. "That's my favorite movie."

"No shit?" he repeats with a smirk.

"No shit," she says.

He tells her that he spent two days in Dublin, a day in Bath, a day in Oxford, a day in Cambridge, and he's rounding out his trip in UK with three days in London.

"Where will you go next?" Kate asks.

"Not sure," Eliot answers. "I'll see where my boss wants me to go next."

He asks Kate what brings her to London besides a weird fascination with Henry's second wife.

"That's actually it," she says. "I'm working on my thesis."

"Thesis?"

"I'm in a PhD program. English history. I'm studying Henry and Anne."

Eliot nods and wonders what he ever thought a girl like Kate would want with a college dropout who now wrote for a travel blog.

She continues to explain that she's spending a semester researching in England. One of the benefits of her particular program, she says. While she tells him about secondary sources versus primary sources, he struggles to rip his eyes from the bright pink bra peeking out from the slightly sheer black dress.

"It must be awesome to be a travel blogger," she says.

"It is," he says, "but my job also means the worst sleeping quarters in the whole of London."

Kate laughs and says, "This is utter bullshit, Eliot."

"What do you mean?" he asks, putting on his most innocent facial expression.

"I did *not* agree to go home with you tonight," she says.

"I didn't ask," he says. "All I said was that I have the worst sleeping quarters in all of London. In fact, one could argue that you're clearly insisting that we go home together because you are the one who said it."

She shakes her head. "You are something else, Eliot."

They have another drink and order chips. Kate comments on how she loves British-isms because they make her feel like she's from another time even though she *knows* they're just modern colloquialisms like they have in America.

"Do you want to get out of here?" Eliot asks. "Get better acquainted maybe?"

Kate smirks and for a second, he worries that she's going to say no.

"Yeah," she says. "Let's go."

They walk outside and Eliot dials a cab on his cell phone.

They slide into the backseat of the black car that looks almost normal except for the cab driver's credentials prominently displayed and Eliot tells him the name of the hostel he's staying at.

During the fifteen minute cab ride back to Eliot's hostel, they speak only a few words about the beauty of the city at night. The air, full of the smoke from the driver's cigarette, is heavy with the unspoken promises as Eliot entangles their fingers.

"Here you go, kids," the driver says. Eliot hands him a few colorful bills and thanks him for the ride.

"So this is a hostel," Kate says. "I've always wanted to see one."

They walk in the front door and he greets the front desk attendant.

"Hey, Eliot," the guy says.

"Hi, Frank," Eliot says. "Anyone in room three?"

Frank smiles. "Nope. I'll be sure to keep them down here a little while longer, eh?"

"Thanks," Eliot says. He can feel a blush creep across his face and he silently curses the pale skin that shows his every emotion.

"This is quaint," Kate says as they walk up the stairs covered in stained carpet to the third floor. "I don't know what I thought a hostel would be but I'm not sure this is it."

"What were you expecting?" he asks. "Perpetual orgies?"

She giggles. "Something like that."

They arrive at room three. He tries to open the door but his hands shake so much that he fumbles with the room key for a full thirty-five seconds before finding the equilibrium that allows him to lead Kate into his room.

"Sorry," he mutters.

"Don't worry about it," she says. "We all get that way when we've had a few."

He murmurs an agreement but knows that his shakiness has nothing to do with how many drinks he had.

"This is adorable," Kate announces, putting her denim jacket on the coat rack next to the door.

Eliot drops his keys and wallet on a dresser, thinking that *adorable* is the last way that he would ever describe his hostel room. Six bunk beds with worn green comforters and orange shag carpets that had likely not been truly clean since they were purchased, probably in the 1970's, were not his definition of *adorable*.

Kate asks if he minds that she turn the light off because she has never been a fan of artificial lighting.

In the dark, he finds his way through the haze of too many ales to pull off her slightly sheer black dress and wrench off his wrinkled khakis. He struggles to unhook the bright pink bra but his hands won't cooperate.

"I've got it," she says softly. "Get a condom."

He asks if she's sure, because they did meet in Soho and was she sure that she was actually interested in men?

"Seriously, Eliot?" Kate says with a laugh. "You're going to ask me this when I'm naked?"

"I just thought about it," he says. "And you know how much you like Anne Boleyn."

When she pulls his mouth to hers, he guides himself into her and tries to find the coherence to remember the exact feeling of being enveloped by the warmth and passion.

Kate digs fingernails into his back and bites his shoulder. "Fuck," she says, "I'm close."

"Tell me what you need," he says.

"Faster," she says.

He moves quicker, deeper and Kate cries out. Soon after, he can no longer think about anything other than her and lets himself go, collapsing on her when he finishes.

At some point, he rolls off of her and removes the condom. He falls asleep with Kate in his arms, her head on his chest and her long hair tickling his arms.

His alarm goes off around seven, a reminder that he has to get going if he is going to hit every sight he needs to. He reaches for Kate but catches only air in his fingers.

He wonders if he dreamt her but catches a glimpse in the mirror of scratches on his back and a bite mark on his shoulder. He tries to recall the feeling of her skin, the way that her hair felt on his chest, but he can no longer remember.

Becca Wagner is a twentysomething Carrie Bradshaw wannabe who lives in upstate New York. She spends most of her spare time watching Sex and the City or murder shows, singing karaoke, and pretending that she's going to write more.

Be Careful What You Wish For

Jennifer R. Donohue

I thought it would be easier to shop with a picture of the list on my phone, but it had gotten out of hand. I stood in the center of an aisle, staring at my screen like a total novice, trying to interpret every item. Dog food was easiest. "Jesse's girl" was a joke, but eye of newt was a real one. Why wouldn't it be here by the frog legs? Wait, did we need frog legs too?

"Did you need help with something?" I hadn't met the clerk before, and her nametag was still handwritten, Debbie. Apprentices got their official nametags if they made it six months. I'd seen only a handful of those in my years coming to this store.

"Are you out of eye of newt?" I asked.

"Wow, that's an oldie," Debbie said, wide eyed. I flared my nostrils minutely, and she hurried to add "No, no, we're not out, we just keep them in the warmer part of the store. Something over here was making them freeze, and frozen then thawed eyes of newt is terrible, it's like frozen and thawed tomatoes. They look okay and then when you go to use them something awful happens instead."

"Okay, thanks." I followed Debbie; salamander items were there too, and if I'd thought of that I wouldn't have needed apprentice help. Also phoenix feathers, in locked metal boxes with anti theft devices on them, each box engraved with which generation of Phoenix it had come from.

"Is there anything else? It looks like you have quite the list." These phones, they have such huge screens nowadays.

"Oh, no, most of this stuff is jokes. Unless you actually know where D. B. Cooper's treasure is."

"Nope, just Blackbeard. Though I guess everybody knows where the treasure *is*, just not how to safely get past the booby traps," she said cheerfully. Maybe Debbie would make it after all.

"Any unicorn horn?" If I was getting into impulse buys, I might as well aim high.

"No, the unicorn horn market has all but dried up. People keep trying to pass narwhal horns, and that works for the trophy hunters, but you and I both know they're very different things."

"Then I'll just grab some bread and milk and be on my way."

"Alrighty. Giant's bread or regular? And what sort of milk?" I blinked; there was such a thing as *too* helpful. If the store didn't have a standing 'no dogs rule but the owner's dog' rule, ours would be staring at each other by now, picking up on everything unsaid.

"Those I don't need help finding. Thanks." The bell at the entryway rang, grabbing Debbie's attention and allowing me to escape back to the coolers.

I picked cow's milk because the other varieties tasted really weird on cereal. I didn't want giant's bread because really, there's only so much bone meal you want in your grilled cheese sandwiches. Oh cheese, I needed cheese. And probably oil. That was the kind of thing that never made it onto the list, but the bottle always seemed nearly done.

The display of olive oil never had the same bottles twice; most of the time it was that sort of Greek and/or Roman mythology motif, or even just normal bottles like from a perfectly mundane store, and this time they seemed more, I didn't know, Middle Eastern? They looked like oil lamps instead, and I picked one up and turned it this way and that, looking for a label. It was easy to get something that wasn't as it seemed. I found something on it that looked like a smudged label, or maybe it just said the country of origin on it, and smeared at the spot with my thumb.

Even as the smoke started to emanate from the lamp spout, I knew the mistake I'd made. The olive oil was probably over by the wine again or something. This kind of thing was to be expected in a store with high turnover, but still.

The genie crossed his arms and looked at me, the platonic ideal of what you'd expect a lamp genie to look like, pointed beard and mustache. Bronzed skin. But I didn't need him, and I'd crossed my own arms impatiently while I waited for him to manifest. "I have the power to grant you three wishes, but there are—"

"But there are rules, yeah, I got it. The thing is, I'm not buying you, and the owner would be pissed if I just took your wishes gratis, so can we forget I did this and move on with our lives?"

"There are rules," he said, perturbed at the interruption. "You are the owner of the lamp."

"No, I'm not. I didn't buy the lamp, I just performed an action which you clearly construed as rubbing."

"Oh, those are on wholesale this week, $49.99," Debbie chirped, at my elbow again.

"Such a bargain," I said, and rolled my eyes. "You need to fix the signs."

"I'm so sorry," Debbie said, and her cheery façade cracked. She realized the implications, of course. It was the genie who had a hard time getting himself up to speed. "Maybe...we can do a payment plan? Or wait, are you a member? What am I asking you have to be a member. Do you have your coupon book with you?" She didn't look around for the owner, but little passed under this roof that the lady of the house didn't know about. *Her* dog was allowed in.

"Yes, I have my coupon book, but that isn't the point. I'm not in the market for genies or wishes or the ugly empty lamps they leave behind. They're worse than hermit crabs."

"That's only if you use your third wish to—" Debbie began.

I sighed. "I know that. Most people in good conscience use their third wish to free the genie. It's probably why this whole genie trapped in a lamp granting wishes thing perpetuates, otherwise why would they agree to it? When they get freed, they don't have to go back to the lamp *or* to wherever genie land is, they get to stay here."

"Oh. I wonder if my landlord...." Debbie trailed off, looking from me to the genie again, squared her shoulders in almost comical resolve. "Mr. Genie, sir, you're just going to have to go back into your lamp. This customer is saying she didn't rub you on purpose and so you don't owe her anything."

"I'm not supposed to be here?" the genie asked slowly. Probably trying to keep his rules in mind. Genies actually had thousands of rules, if not millions, but very few of them applied to the intersection of genie and human life. Or genie and witch life, et cetera.

"Exactly, you're not supposed to be here. There's no rule that says you can't go back into your lamp if you prematurely manifested." It was the most confident I'd heard Debbie sound in our very brief acquaintance.

"The lamp was rubbed. I cannot summon myself." Of course that 'premature' word would get him.

"Do the rules have an operational definition of rubbing, because I want to know to the letter what that definition is, if I'm going to be out fifty bucks on a cruddy soon-to-be-empty lamp."

"My lamp is not cruddy," the genie said, and he did sound hurt. This might be unprecedented, which meant this had to be handled delicately if Debbie couldn't just steamroll him. I wasn't about to pull out some chalk and banish him; uninvited spell work was a worse rule to break than the dog one.

"But it is unwanted," I said. "And I didn't mean to handle your lamp in such a manner that would be considered rubbing."

"I do not understand how wishes could be unwanted," he said in the same tone. Goddess save me from puppy eyed genies and their lamps. Debbie had evidently used up all her resolve and stood wringing her hands, looking from me to the genie and back again.

"Sometimes people are satisfied with what they have. Or they know the risk of wishes. Everything has its price."

"You do know the rules," the genie said appreciatively.

"I told you I did. And there we have it. I officially refuse the service of your wishes, and thus you must return to your lamp as soon as you are able to wait for the next rubber. Preferably one who's signed up for this nonsense."

The genie looked at Debbie, who was avoiding eye contact, and back to me. "If you refuse my service, I can't make you take it. I shall return to my lamp."

I nodded. "Good."

It wasn't until I was on my way home that I realized I never picked up the cheese.

Jennifer R. Donohue grew up at the Jersey Shore and now lives in central New York with her husband and her Doberman. Though she got a Bachelor's degree in psychology, she has always wanted to write, and is now both a Codexian and an Associate member of the SFWA. She works at the Huntington Memorial Library, where she started HML Writers in 2014. Her work has appeared in Daily Science Fiction, Mythic Delirum, Syntax & Salt, Escape Pod, and elsewhere. She blogs at Authorized Musings, where she shares fiction and the tribulations of the writing life, and tweets @AuthorizedMusin. This story first appeared on Jennifer's Patreon in 2018